THE WALKING DEAD™

BOOK EIGHT

a continuing story of survival horror.

created by Robert Kirkman

image comics presents

The Walking Dead
book eight

ROBERT KIRKMAN
creator, writer

CHARLIE ADLARD
penciler, inker, cover

CLIFF RATHBURN
gray tones

RUS WOOTON
letterer

SINA GRACE
editor

Original series covers by
CHARLIE ADLARD & CLIFF RATHBURN

SKYBOUND
www.skybound.com

Robert Kirkman
chief executive officer

J.J. Didde
president

Sina Grace
editorial director

Shawn Kirkham
director of business development

Tim Daniel
digital content manager

Chad Manion
assistant to mr. grace

Sydney Pennington
assistant to mr. kirkham

Feldman Public Relations LA
public relations

image
www.imagecomics.com

Robert Kirkman
chief operating officer

Erik Larsen
chief financial officer

Todd McFarlane
president

Marc Silvestri
chief executive officer

Jim Valentino
vice-president

Eric Stephenson
publisher

Todd Martinez
sales & licensing coordinator

Jennifer de Guzman
pr & marketing director

Branwyn Bigglestone
accounts manager

Emily Miller
administrative assistant

Jamie Parreno
marketing assistant

Sarah deLaine
events coordinator

Kevin Yuen
digital rights coordinator

Tyler Shainline
production manager

Drew Gill
art director

Jonathan Chan
design director

Monica Garcia
production artist

Vincent Kukua
production artist

Jana Cook
production artist

THE WALKING DEAD, BOOK EIGHT. First Printing. Published by Image Comics, Inc., Office of publication: 2134 Allston Way, 2nd Floor, Berkeley, California 94704. PRINTED IN CANADA. ISBN: 978-1-60706-593-7

For international rights inquiries, please contact foreign@skybound.com.

Chapter Fifteen: We Find Ourselves

FUCK.

UNGH.

THIS IS GOING TO TAKE FUCKING FOREVER...

I THINK IT'S TIME TO START ANOTHER BURN PILE.
THERE'S ROOM OVER NEAR RICK'S HOUSE-- AND LOTS OF BODIES THERE.

OKAY, JUST KEEP IT CLOSE TO THE CENTER OF THE ROAD--AWAY FROM THE YARDS.
WILL DO.

MOTHER FUCK.

UNGH...

ABRAHAM...

GAK.

WRAAUGH.

GET RID OF HER BEFORE RICK SEES IT.

I--I DON'T--

GOD DAMN IT.

BLAM!

FUCKING MAKE ME DO *EVERYTHING*.
JESUS.

WHERE *IS* RICK ANYWAY?

DON'T KNOW...
PROBABLY STILL WITH CARL.

IT'S BEEN NEARLY TWENTY-FOUR HOURS, RICK.
PLEASE, EAT SOMETHING.

NOT HUNGRY.

OKAY THEN...

SHE JUST WANTED TO SAVE HER SON...

WHAT?

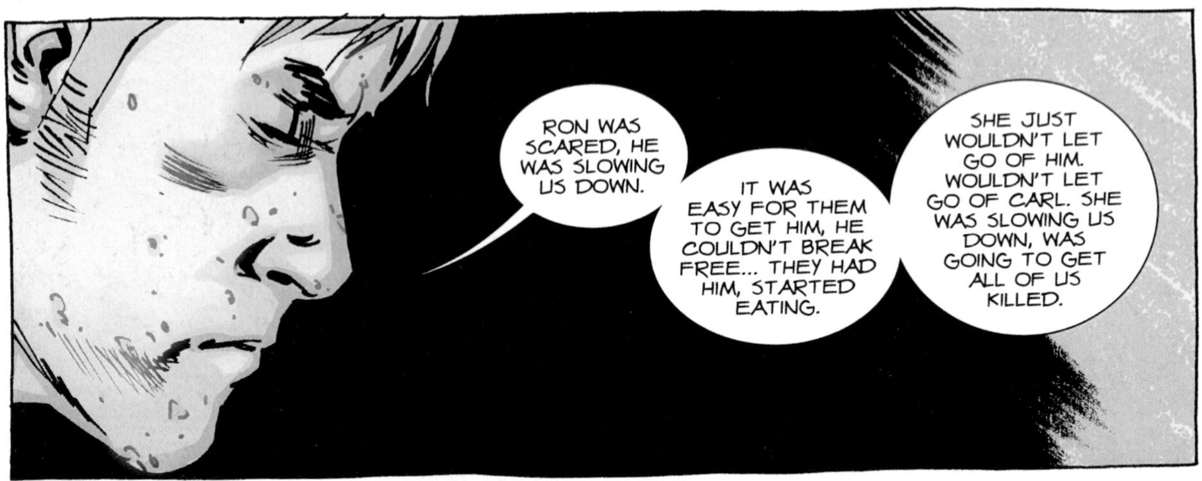
RON WAS SCARED, HE WAS SLOWING US DOWN.
IT WAS EASY FOR THEM TO GET HIM, HE COULDN'T BREAK FREE... THEY HAD HIM, STARTED EATING.
SHE JUST WOULDN'T LET GO OF HIM. WOULDN'T LET GO OF CARL. SHE WAS SLOWING US DOWN, WAS GOING TO GET ALL OF US KILLED.

WHAT ARE YOU SAYING?

I DID WHAT I HAD TO DO.
WHAT SHE *MADE* ME HAVE TO DO.

RICK, STOP.
PLEASE.

SHE WAS PULLING ON CARL. SHE WAS SCARED, SHE COULDN'T LET GO... THEY HAD HER.
BUT SHE WAS HOLDING US BACK.

I HACKED OFF HER HAND.
THERE WAS NO OTHER CHOICE.

I KNOW WHAT THAT FEELS LIKE.
I DIDN'T WANT TO DO IT.

I CAN'T BELIEVE JESSIE IS GONE.
I REALLY LIKED HER.

AND THEN CARL WAS SHOT...
...TO THINK EVERYTHING MAY HAVE BEEN FOR NOTHING.

I'M SORRY, DENISE. I DON'T MEAN TO...

IT'S OKAY...

PLEASE, CAN YOU JUST... KEEP THAT BETWEEN YOU AND ME?
NO NEED TO SCARE ANYONE.
OH, OF COURSE.

UNGH.

LET ME TAKE IT FROM HERE. WE'RE NEARLY DONE FOR THE NIGHT ANYWAY... YOU GET SOME REST.
NO, I'M NOT QUITTING EARLY. I'M FINE..

ANDREA?

SPENCER.
WHAT DO YOU **WANT?**

I WAS WONDERING... IF YOU MIGHT WANT TO GET TOGETHER LATER TONIGHT?

I DON'T KNOW...
AND I WOULDN'T WANT TO TALK ABOUT THAT RIGHT NOW ANYWAY.

YEAH, UH... I UNDERSTAND.
SORRY ABOUT THAT.
LET ME HELP YOU...

I NEED TO GET BACK OUT THERE. SORRY.
NONSENSE, GLENN. IT'LL BE DARK SOON. THEY'RE ALREADY STARTING TO QUIT. YOU CAN JUST STAY PUT.

OKAY, YOU TWISTED MY ARM.

I'M SO GLAD YOU'RE BACK HERE... I WAS SO WORRIED AND I--
OH, GOD.

MAGGIE, WHAT'S WRONG?
IT'S NOTHING, JUST...

AFTER EVERYTHING I'VE BEEN THROUGH... ALL THE BAD THAT'S HAPPENED. I ACTUALLY FEEL LUCKY RIGHT NOW... I'M HAPPY...
...AND THAT FEELS SO WRONG, WITH EVERYONE WHO DIED...

SURVIVOR'S GUILT... TRUST ME, I'VE HAD IT. IT'S ONLY NATURAL TO FEEL GUILTY FOR BEING HAPPY.
BUT... I FEEL THE EXACT SAME WAY. I LOVE YOU, MAGGIE.

WHAT A GODDAMN DAY. AM I RIGHT?
SHIT FUCK.

ROSITA? WHAT'S GOT YOU SO LOST IN THOUGHT?

OH, SORRY.
I'M JUST TRYING TO DECIDE IF ENOUGH TIME HAS PASSED...

IF ENOUGH TIME HAS PASSED FOR WHAT?

FOR ME TO ADMIT THAT I KNOW YOU'VE BEEN FUCKING HOLLY.

...

THEY WILL ALL BE MISSED.

WE'VE BEEN GOING AT THIS ALL WRONG.

OR RATHER, I'VE BEEN GOING AT THIS ALL WRONG.

SOMETIMES I EVEN THOUGHT I WAS BETTER OFF *ALONE.*
I CAN'T BELIEVE HOW STUPID I'VE BEEN.

THE RESOURCES SPENT... THE PERSONAL CONFLICTS... I'VE ALWAYS BEEN WARY ABOUT BEING PARTS OF THESE BIG GROUPS.
SAFETY IN NUMBERS... THAT'S WHAT KEPT ME AROUND.
BUT I NEVER REALLY THOUGHT ABOUT THE TRUE POTENTIAL OF OUR LITTLE COMMUNITY.

I THINK ABOUT WHAT WE CAN ACCOMPLISH TOGETHER, NOW THAT I'VE SEEN WHAT WE'RE CAPABLE OF WHEN WE WORK TOGETHER.
GUYS, I GOTTA SAY... MY MIND IS *RACING* WITH THE POSSIBILITIES.

JUST THINKING ABOUT THE EASY STUFF FIRST... WE COULD USE CARS AND OTHER THINGS TO CREATE AN OBSTACLE FIELD IN THE ROADS LEADING TO US.
A MAZE TO SLOW DOWN ROAMERS AND BLOCK UNWANTED VEHICLES FROM APPROACHING US BEFORE WE'RE AWARE OF THEM.
ANY OTHER IDEAS?

WE COULD MAKE THE WALLS MORE SECURE BY PACKING DIRT AGAINST THE INSIDE OF THEM...
WE COULD GET THAT DIRT FROM DIGGING SOME TRENCHES AROUND THE PERIMETER OF OUR AREA--NOTHING HUGE, JUST SOMETHING DEEP ENOUGH TO TRIP UP A ROAMER WHEN THEY TRY TO WALK THROUGH IT.

IF THAT DIRT WAS HIGH ENOUGH BEHIND THE WALLS, WE COULD ACTUALLY PUT A WALKWAY AROUND THE TOP. THAT WOULD ALLOW US TO STAND AT THE TOP OF THE FENCE AND TAKE CARE OF ANY ROAMERS WITHOUT LEAVING.

PROBABLY NOT A BAD IDEA FOR ALL OF US TO GO BACK TO WEARING OUR WEAPONS AT ALL TIMES--AND I COULD HELP TRAIN PEOPLE TO USE THEM.

THIS IS ALL GOOD. THIS IS WHAT WE NEED... WE NEED TO BE *THINKING.*
IF WE REALLY SPEND TIME ON THIS, I KNOW WE CAN COME UP WITH SOME REALLY GOOD WAYS TO PROTECT OURSELVES--AND MAKE THIS A SAFER PLACE TO LIVE.
I THINK WE SHOULD MEET LIKE THIS REGULARLY FROM NOW ON.
ANYTHING ELSE, GUYS?

I'M DONE RECRUITING NEW PEOPLE. IT'S TOO DANGEROUS. WE'D BE MUCH BETTER SERVED HELPING TO IMPROVE WHAT WE HAVE HERE.

IF WE TOOK MORE PEOPLE ON SUPPLY RUNS, WE WOULD BE ABLE TO GO FURTHER, MAYBE STAY OUT OVER NIGHT AND HIT AREAS WE HAVEN'T REACHED YET...

I THINK IT MIGHT BE GOOD TO HAVE MORE... COMMUNITY EVENTS. I KNOW THERE'S A LOT OF PEOPLE HERE I CAN'T EVEN NAME. I'D LIKE TO KNOW EVERYONE.

MORE GOOD SUGGESTIONS. AND THINKING LONG-TERM HERE--AS WE MAKE OUR COMMUNITY FAIL SAFE... ONCE WE'RE SECURE HERE, THERE'S NOTHING KEEPING US FROM EXPANDING OUR SAFE ZONE OUT... BLOCKING OFF MORE LAND, GIVING US MORE SPACE TO LIVE IN, TO FARM, ANYTHING.
SO FAR, OUR EFFORTS HAVE BEEN TOWARD SURVIVING, MAKING IT ONE MORE DAY, ONE MORE WEEK.

NOW I WANT TO LEAVE THAT BEHIND... FOCUS MORE ON WHAT WE REALLY WANT... RE-ESTABLISHED CIVILIZATION.
THAT'S WHAT WE SHOULD BE WORKING TOWARD... AND I THINK THE VERY FIRST STEPS TOWARD THAT HAVE BEEN TAKEN HERE TODAY.

ROSITA? WHAT ARE YOU DOING?
I'M *LEAVING.*
I'M TRYING TO GET PAST IT... BUT I CAN'T. OKAY?

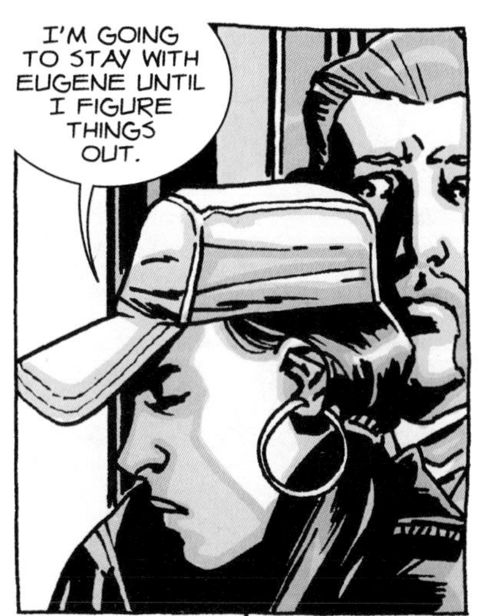
I'M GOING TO STAY WITH EUGENE UNTIL I FIGURE THINGS OUT.

I'M SORRY FOR WHAT I...
I'M SORRY.

OH, I HADN'T REALIZED. THAT MAKES IT ALL BETTER.
ASSHOLE.

WAIT. *LISTEN.*
I'M NOT SORRY FOR CHEATING ON YOU WITH HOLLY. I'M SORRY THAT I HURT YOU IN THE PROCESS. AFTER MY WIFE DIED... YOU WERE THERE FOR ME. I APPRECIATE THAT.
AND FOR A TIME, YOU WERE... WHAT I *NEEDED.*
BUT I ALWAYS FOUND MYSELF THINKING *"WHAT IF YOU AREN'T THE LAST WOMAN ON EARTH?"*
AND, WELL... YOU'RE NOT.

FUCK YOU!

SLAM!

EVERYONE SEEMS ON BOARD WITH MY PLANS. I THINK WE'RE GOING TO BE ABLE TO MAKE THIS WORK.
IT'S HARD... BEING OPTIMISTIC WITH YOU HERE... LIKE THIS.
I'M DOING IT FOR YOU, CARL. I'M TRYING TO THINK OF YOUR FUTURE AND...

WHY AM I DOING THIS? YOU CAN'T HEAR ME.
YOU'RE PROBABLY--
RICK?

I'M SORRY, ANDREA. COME IN.
I'M JUST...

WHATEVER IT IS, I UNDERSTAND. DON'T APOLOGIZE.
BROUGHT YOU SOME FOOD.

THANK YOU, BUT... I'M NOT EATING MUCH THESE DAYS.
ANY CHANGE?
NONE.

DOESN'T MEAN ANYTHING. HE'S ALIVE. HE'S HEALING.
HE'LL GET BETTER. YOU'LL SEE, RICK. YOU JUST HAVE TO REMAIN POSITIVE.

IT'S HARD, I CAN'T SHAKE THIS FEELING... NO MATTER HOW HARD I TRY.

I CAN'T PICTURE HIM WAKING UP. I CAN'T IMAGINE TALKING TO HIM EVER AGAIN. I JUST CAN'T SEE IT.
ANDREA..
I THINK CARL IS GOING TO DIE.

KOFF!
NG.

CARL?!
CAN YOU HEAR ME?!

CARL?

CARL?
CAN YOU HEAR ME?

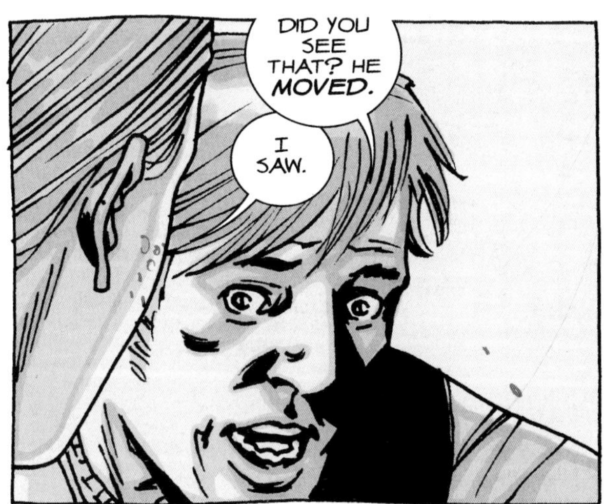
DID YOU SEE THAT? HE *MOVED.*
I SAW.

HE BARELY TWITCHED. I'M SORRY, RICK... BUT HE'S STILL NOT OPENING HIS EYE, HE'S NOT COMING OUT OF IT.

I'M JUST GLAD I DIDN'T IMAGINE IT.
HOLD ON.

CARL MOVED!

WHAT DO YOU MEAN, *MOVED?*

HE LIFTED HIS HEAD, COUGHED.
WHAT DOES IT MEAN?!

COULD MEAN ANYTHING, COULD MEAN NOTHING. COULD YOU... LEAVE FOR A MOMENT?
I'M SORRY, I JUST WANT TO CHECK OUT A FEW THINGS, BEST IF I'M NOT DISTRACTED.
PLEASE.

RICK...

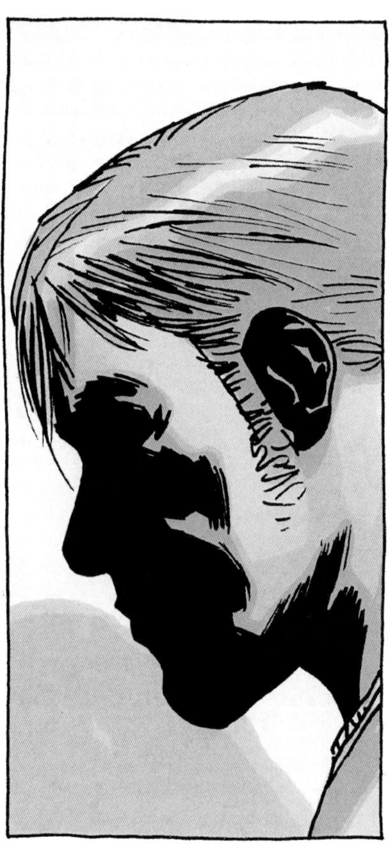

I'M FINE.

YOU WANT ANYTHING TO DRINK? WATER?
YES, THANK YOU.

OKAY...

HOW IS HE? IS EVERYTHING OKAY?
HE'S STABLE.

HE'S STILL IN THE COMA. I DON'T KNOW WHAT YOU SAW, BUT IT'S NOT UNCOMMON FOR COMATOSE PATIENTS TO HAVE BRIEF SPONTANEOUS MOVEMENTS.
IT'S NOT A GOOD OR BAD SIGN. AND HE'S NOT WAKING UP. UNFORTUNATELY.
YOU NEED TO REMEMBER, A GOOD-SIZED PORTION OF HIS HEAD WAS DAMAGED. LIKE I TOLD YOU, NO SEVERE TRAUMA TO THE BRAIN, HE WAS LUCKY... BUT THIS ISN'T SOMETHING WHERE...
LISTEN... HE'S NOT OUT OF THE WOODS YET.

AND WHEN HE DOES WAKE UP, WE DON'T YET KNOW WHAT CONDITION HE'LL BE IN...

KNOCK! KNOCK!
I'M COMING, HOLD ON!

UH...

EUGENE?
HI... UM... WHAT'S THE MATTER?

NOTHING, I JUST... I WASN'T EXPECTING ANYONE.
WHAT DO YOU WANT, ROSITA?

WHAT DOES IT LOOK LIKE I WANT?
I NEED A PLACE TO STAY FOR A WHILE.

WHAT?
WHY?

WILL YOU JUST LET ME IN ALREADY?
SURE, BUT... WHAT HAPPENED?

I HAD TO GET AWAY FROM ABRAHAM BEFORE I KILL HIM.
HE'S FUCKING HOLLY, IF YOU CAN BELIEVE IT.

OH, I HAD NO IDEA... I'M SO SORRY.
YOU... CAN STAY HERE AS LONG AS YOU'D LIKE. BUT... WHY HERE... WITH ME?

DON'T MAKE THIS AWKWARD, OKAY?
YOU KNOW WHY.

NO, I DON'T.
LOOK, THINGS HAVE BEEN TENSE SINCE WE LEARNED YOU LIED TO US ALL THAT TIME--SO WE'D PROTECT YOU... BUT THAT DOESN'T REALLY CHANGE ANYTHING...
YOU'RE THE ONLY FRIEND I HAVE HERE.
OKAY?

RICK?

RICK, IT'S LATE AND... THERE'S NOTHING YOU CAN DO HERE--NO REASON FOR YOU TO BE HERE. PLEASE, IF HE WAKES UP I'LL COME GET YOU MYSELF.
JUST GO HOME AND GET SOME SLEEP. THIS ISN'T GOOD FOR YOU.

IF IT'S ALL THE SAME TO YOU, I'D REALLY LIKE TO STAY AND--

EVERYTHING OKAY?

I'M SORRY, I DIDN'T KNOW...
I'LL... GET OUT OF YOUR HAIR.

HEY.

OH, SORRY.

DON'T BE.
I SAW YOU BETWEEN THE HOUSES-- BUT COULDN'T QUITE MAKE YOU OUT.
DIDN'T MEAN TO INTRUDE.

IT'S OKAY. TOO COLD TO BE DOING THIS ANYWAY.

MORGAN
I MISS HIM, TOO. MORGAN REALLY HELPED ME EARLY ON... HE WAS A GOOD MAN.

I FEEL LIKE I DIDN'T GET TO TALK TO HIM ENOUGH NEAR THE END... WITH EVERYTHING THAT WAS GOING ON... BUT STILL, I WISH I'D BEEN ABLE TO SAY GOODBYE.

TRUST ME. YOU DON'T.
IT WASN'T... IT'S NOT RIGHT... WATCHING THEM COME BACK.

YEAH.

WAS WORSE WITH MORGAN SOMEHOW. I WASN'T KIND TO HIM... BUT I WAS TRYING, I THINK I'D PUT THAT BEHIND ME.
POINT IS, I FELT LIKE I WAS BUILDING SOMETHING WITH MORGAN. IT WASN'T JUST SEX, IT WASN'T JUST COMPANIONSHIP.
I WANTED A LIFE WITH HIM.

ISN'T THAT FUNNY...?

NOT AT ALL, I THINK THAT'S WHAT EVERYONE WANTS.

NO, I MEAN... AFTER EVERYTHING THAT'S HAPPENED, WHY WOULD I THINK THAT--THAT I COULD BE HAPPY? IT'S LIKE YOU AND JESSIE...
WHAT'S WRONG WITH US?

...
ANYWAY... IT'S LATE.

THE TANGLE OF CARS SHOULD START HERE. THEY'D BE JUST FAR ENOUGH APART FOR SOMEONE TO WEAVE THROUGH QUICKLY IF THEY WERE BEING CHASED, BUT SO CLOSE A ROAMER WOULD BE UNABLE TO MAKE THEIR WAY THROUGH.
THIS TRENCH, IN FRONT OF THE LINE OF CARS... OR *BEHIND* THEM?

WHY NOT BOTH? WE'LL NEED THE DIRT TO SUPPORT THE WALL.
MAY TAKE SOME TIME... BUT WORTH IT IN THE END.

TIME IS NOT AN ISSUE. THAT'S THE POINT OF THIS. I WANT TO BE LIVING HERE WITH CARL WHEN HE'S IN HIS THIRTIES... LET'S START MAKING PLANS FOR THAT.
I DON'T CARE IF IT'LL TAKE TEN YEARS... IF IT'S A GOOD IDEA, WE DO IT.

THAT'S GOOD TO KNOW. IT'S GOOD TO HEAR THAT YOU'RE THINKING MORE LONG TERM WITH--
BLAM! BLAM!

STAY PUT--DON'T MOVE. I'LL BE RIGHT BACK.

GOOD JOB, MAGGIE, KEEP THAT ELBOW STRAIGHT.
BLAM! BLAM!

I FORGOT YOU WERE OUT HERE, ANDREA. WE WERE TAKING A TOUR, TRYING TO MAP OUT OUR NEW DEFENSES.
HOW MUCH LONGER ARE YOU GOING TO BE AT IT?
WE SHOULDN'T BE WALKING OUT HERE WHEN STRAY BULLETS ARE WHIZZING BY.

WHY IN THE WORLD NOT?
SERIOUSLY, THOUGH-- WE JUST RELOADED, BUT WE CAN STOP AT ANY TIME.

ACTUALLY, MIGHT WANT TO FIRE OFF A FEW MORE SHOTS...

OKAY, TIME FOR A LITTLE ON THE JOB TRAINING.
WE'VE GOT SOME DISTANCE BETWEEN US AND THEM... STAY CALM, MAKE YOUR SHOTS COUNT.
DON'T PANIC AND TAKE OUT THOSE ROAMERS!

I'M NOT READY FOR THIS!

THEN **GET** READY. THIS IS LIFE OR DEATH, OLIVIA-- DEFEND YOURSELVES.
GO!

BLAM!
BLAM!
BLAM!

SPAK!
SPLAGG!

SPAKK!

SPAK!

BLAM!

GOOD EFFORT, EVERYONE-- BUT SAVE YOUR BULLETS.
I'LL TAKE IT FROM HERE.

BLAM!

BLAM!

BLAM!

BLAM!

BLAM!

LET THEM IN CLOSE IF YOU CAN MANAGE. IT MAKES THEM MUCH EASIER TARGETS.
GRUH...

BLAM!

AND THAT, LADIES AND GENTLEMEN, IS WHY ANDREA IS HEADING UP OUR GUN TRAINING.
WOW.

POINT AND SHOOT, IT'S NOT HARD...
...AND YOU'VE GOT ALL THE INCENTIVE IN THE WORLD TO GET IT RIGHT.

AND I THINK THAT'S JUST ENOUGH GUNFIRE TO MAKE THINGS OUT HERE INTERESTING.
LET'S PACK IT IN BEFORE A SWARM OF ROAMERS CUT US OFF FROM THE FENCE.

EVERYONE ALL RIGHT?
YEAH. A LITTLE ROAMER ACTION, THINK WE SHOULD PACK IT INSIDE FOR NOW, CONTINUE OUR SCOUTING OF THE AREA TOMORROW.

HEADING UP THE GUN TRAINING. YOU... **TEACHING.** CAN YOU BELIEVE IT?
I KNOW, RIGHT?

I THINK BACK TO THOSE DAYS, FIRST TIME I FIRED A GUN... HOW **ALIEN** IT FELT.
I KEEP THINKING, WHAT WOULD SHANE SAY IF HE COULD SEE ME NOW?

SHIT, I'M SORRY, RICK. I KNOW HOW...
I DIDN'T MEAN TO...

NO, IT'S FINE. REALLY. THINGS GOT... **HORRIBLE.** BUT YOU KNOW, SHANE WAS MY OLDEST... MY **BEST** FRIEND.
IF I'M HONEST, DESPITE ALL THAT HAPPENED, WHAT HE TRIED TO DO TO ME... I STILL MISS HIM.
BUT THE FACT IS... I REALLY JUST DON'T THINK ABOUT HIM A LOT... AT ALL... EVER.

I DON'T REALLY THINK ABOUT THE PAST... IT'S TOO PAINFUL.
WELL, YOU KNOW... MY GOD... THE THINGS WE'VE ENDURED.

YEAH. YOU CAN GET CAUGHT UP IN DWELLING ON ALL THE HORRIBLE THINGS THAT HAVE HAPPENED...
...IT CAN SLOW YOU DOWN, GET YOU KILLED.

EXACTLY. SO I JUST DON'T DO IT... I RARELY STOP AND REFLECT ON ANYTHING THAT'S HAPPENED.
DOESN'T MEAN I DON'T MISS LORI, I DO--I JUST CAN'T... THINK ABOUT HER TOO MUCH OR IT'S...

IT'S OKAY.
I GET IT.

IT'S JUST, I'M SO ACCUSTOMED TO LIVING IN THE MOMENT, DAY BY DAY, NOT LOOKING AHEAD, NOT LOOKING BACK...
I WAS BLIND TO HOW DIFFICULT THAT MAKES LIFE.

IT EVENTUALLY GETS TO THE POINT WHERE "SAFETY IN NUMBERS" DOESN'T EVEN SEEM PLAUSIBLE DESPITE HOW MUCH SENSE IT MAKES...
...AND I CAN'T EVEN CONSIDER FOR A MINUTE THAT MY INJURED SON MIGHT LIVE, BECAUSE I'M NOT USED TO LOOKING AHEAD.
WHAT IS GOING ON NOW IS ALL THERE IS... AND...

I'M SORRY, I'M NOT EVEN MAKING SENSE ANYMORE.

NO, I FOLLOW.
I GET WHAT YOU'RE TRYING TO SAY.

GOOD.
WE... WE'VE BEEN THROUGH A LOT TOGETHER. AND WELL, IT MEANS A LOT TO ME THAT YOU'VE BEEN THERE FOR ME SO MUCH.

WE'VE BEEN THERE FOR EACH OTHER, RICK.
YEAH, BUT... NOT REALLY.

FOR THE MOST PART I WAS JUST DOING WHATEVER I FELT WOULD KEEP LORI AND CARL SAFE... THAT'S WHAT DROVE MY DECISIONS.
I HAD VERY LITTLE CONSIDERATION FOR THE GROUP. I LIKED YOU ALL, BUT I WAS WILLING TO DO WHATEVER IT TOOK TO PROTECT MY FAMILY.

THAT'S... UNDERSTANDABLE.

NO, THAT'S... *INEXCUSABLE.*
THE THINGS I DID... THE MOVES I MADE. I JUSTIFIED IT BY SAYING IT WAS FOR THE GOOD OF MY FAMILY... BUT REALLY, I WAS OVERLOOKING THE MOST IMPORTANT PART OF SURVIVAL IN THIS WORLD.
COMMUNITY.

PROTECTING THE GROUP PROTECTS CARL IN A BETTER WAY THAN I EVER REALIZED. IT'S LIKE THIS NEW BARRIER WE'RE TALKING ABOUT OUTSIDE THE FENCE. PROTECT THE FENCE AND MAKE IT THAT MUCH MORE SECURE BY DESIGN.
THAT'S THE KEY... *THAT'S* HOW WE'RE GOING TO SURVIVE IN THIS WORLD.

SO THINGS ARE GOING TO BE DIFFERENT NOW.
I'M GOING TO BE A BETTER PERSON.

I DON'T DOUBT YOU-- BUT HOW CAN YOU BE SO CERTAIN OF THIS? WHAT MAKES YOU THINK THINGS ARE GOING TO GO WELL?

JUST LOOK AT THIS PLACE, ANDREA..

...THIS IS GOING TO WORK.

I HOPE YOU'RE RIGHT.

I *HAVE* TO BE.
IF IT'S NOT WORKING... WE'LL *MAKE* IT WORK.

PICK THIS BACK UP TOMORROW MORNING?
YEP. SEE YOU THEN.

YOU GOING TO CHECK IN ON CARL?
YEAH.
MIND IF I TAG ALONG?

YOU GUYS GOT THIS? MAKE SURE WE'RE ALL LOCKED UP.
YEAH, WE GOT IT COVERED.

ROSITA..

FUCK OFF, ASSHOLE.

I PICKED UP SOME FOOD FOR DINNER. I FIGURED I'D COOK... HAVEN'T DONE THAT IN A WHILE.
SURE.
SOUNDS GREAT.
OH, UM... OKAY.

WHAT WAS THAT? AREN'T THE TWO OF YOU...

WE *WERE*, BUT NOT ANYMORE.
IT'S COMPLICATED.

BUMMER.
YOU DID **NOT** JUST SAY "*BUMMER*."
OH, SHUT UP...
REALLY, GUYS, IT'S NOT AN ISSUE.

YOU'RE STARING AT HER ASS LIKE IT'S AN ISSUE.

SORRY, SORRY... TOOK IT TOO FAR.
DIDN'T MEAN TO BE INSENSITIVE.

HIS HEART RATE IS STEADY, STRONG EVEN, AND HIS VITALS ARE ALL WHERE THEY NEED TO BE.
I'M RELUCTANT TO SAY THIS, WERE I ANSWERING TO A MEDICAL BOARD I'D BE MUCH MORE VAGUE WITH YOU...
...THINGS ARE LOOKING GOOD.
THINGS ARE LOOKING GOOD?
THAT DOESN'T MEAN ANYTHING. HELP ME OUT HERE, DENISE. WHEN IS HE GOING TO WAKE UP?
THE FACT IS, THE EXTENT OF ANY DAMAGE TO HIS BRAIN--IS UNCLEAR.
I'M A SURGEON, BUT NOT A BRAIN SURGEON. BUT HE'S YOUNG, THINGS ARE DIFFERENT WHEN THE BRAIN IS STILL DEVELOPING.
I'M OPTIMISTIC THAT HE WILL WAKE UP... BUT I CAN'T MAKE ANY ASSUMPTIONS AS TO WHEN.
RICK, TAKE AS MUCH TIME AS YOU NEED.
I'M GOING TO MAKE SOME DINNER, I'D LOVE IT IF YOU COULD COME...

HAVEN'T SEEN YOU IN A FEW DAYS.
BEEN BUSY.
AND I SAW YOU *TODAY*.

NOT WHAT I MEANT BY "*SEEN*."

BEEN A LOT GOING ON, HAVEN'T BEEN ABLE TO GET AWAY.
YOU KNOW THAT.

DIDN'T KNOW ROSITA HAD MOVED OUT. WHY DIDN'T YOU TELL ME?
FOUND OUT FROM OLIVIA THAT SHE'D MOVED IN WITH EUGENE. AREN'T YOU LONELY IN THERE?

I'M FUCKING DEALING WITH A LOT HERE, HOLLY.
I NEED A LITTLE *TIME*, OKAY?

YEAH.
FINE.
TAKE ALL THE TIME YOU NEED.

HOLLY, WAIT.

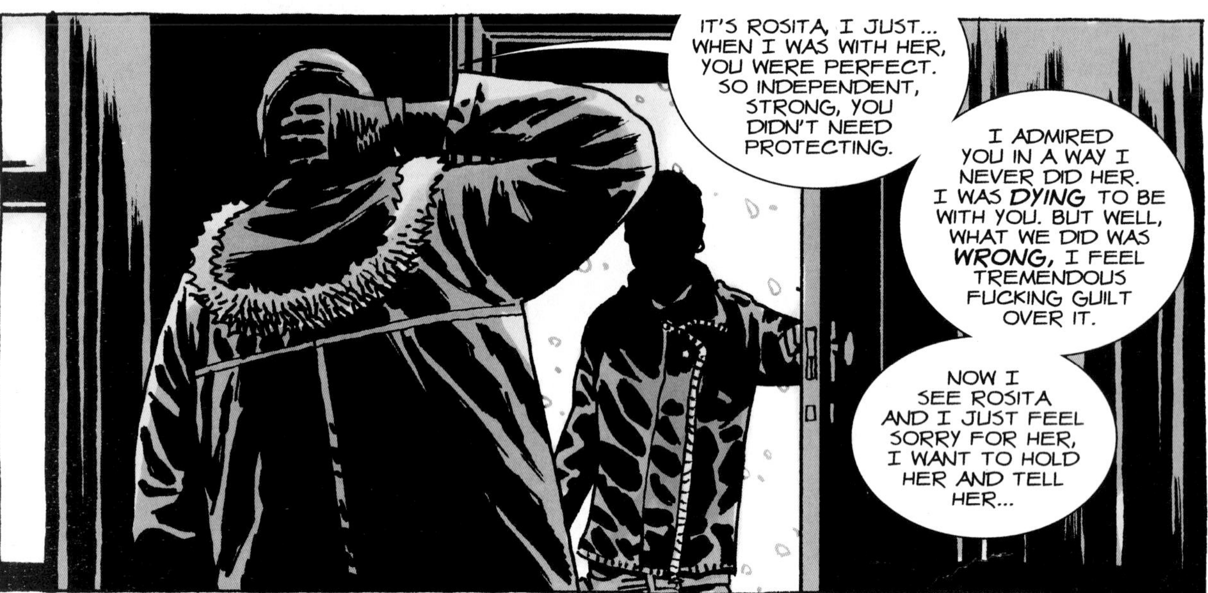
IT'S ROSITA, I JUST... WHEN I WAS WITH HER, YOU WERE PERFECT. SO INDEPENDENT, STRONG, YOU DIDN'T NEED PROTECTING.
I ADMIRED YOU IN A WAY I NEVER DID HER. I WAS DYING TO BE WITH YOU. BUT WELL, WHAT WE DID WAS WRONG, I FEEL TREMENDOUS FUCKING GUILT OVER IT.
NOW I SEE ROSITA AND I JUST FEEL SORRY FOR HER, I WANT TO HOLD HER AND TELL HER...

ARE YOU FUCKING KIDDING ME?!
YOU WANT HER BACK?!

NO. FUCK. THAT'S NOT WHAT I MEAN AT ALL.
IT'S NOT LOVE THAT I FEEL FOR HER... IT'S PITY. I FEEL LIKE I DID HER WRONG AND THAT MAKES ME... FEELING GOOD RIGHT NOW WOULDN'T BE RIGHT.

JUST...
...COME INSIDE.

THANKS FOR THIS.
REALLY.

IT'S REALLY NOTHING.
CAN'T YOU TASTE IT?

IS THIS BEEF JERKY?

IT'S...
...GOOD.

JESSIE
RON

I'M SO SORRY.

IF I KNEW THEN, WHAT I KNOW NOW... YOU'D BOTH BE ALIVE.
I NEVER SHOULD HAVE DRAGGED YOU OUT THERE. I SHOULD HAVE KNOWN RON WOULDN'T BE ABLE TO HANDLE IT.
IT'S EASY TO FORGET THAT NOT EVERY KID IS LIKE CARL...
AND CARL...

...

HELLO?
I CAN'T HELP YOU NOW.

LORI PLEASE! I--I WANT THIS, I NEED TO HEAR YOUR VOICE.
TELL ME...

...THAT THIS WASN'T YOUR FAULT? YOU KNOW I CAN'T DO THAT.
IN FACT, I NEVER WANT TO TALK TO YOU AGAIN.

WHAT?

LOOK AT WHAT YOU LET HAPPEN TO CARL! IT'S ALL YOUR FAULT, JUST LIKE WHAT HAPPENED TO JUDY AND ME! YOU KNOW THAT IT'S TRUE...
IT SHOULD HAVE BEEN YOU THAT GOT SHOT IN THE HEAD!
LORI?

SHUKK!

THUKK!
WHAKK!

ALL CLEAR?
FOR NOW.

ALL CLEAR!

OKAY, PEOPLE... THAT'S THE SIGNAL, LET'S GET TO IT.

YOU SURE YOU'RE UP FOR THIS?
THANKS FOR THE CONCERN, RICK. REST ASSURED, I'LL STOP JUST SHORT OF A HEART ATTACK.
IT'S THE END OF THE WORLD, MIGHT AS WELL DO SOMETHING THAT'LL HELP ME LOSE SOME WEIGHT.

HEY, GLENN?

YEAH?
KEEP AN EYE ON THINGS OUT THERE. YOU KNOW HOW FAST THINGS CAN GET DANGEROUS.
I'M ON IT.

NICE JOB OUT THERE... AS ALWAYS.
THANKS.

HOW YOU HOLDING UP?
YOU OKAY?

OKAY?
I WONDER HOW LONG IT'S GOING TO TAKE FOR YOU TO LEARN TO STOP ASKING THAT QUESTION. ESPECIALLY CONSIDERING THAT YOU ALWAYS KNOW THE ANSWER.

I'M *NOT* OKAY... BUT I'M GETTING BY.
YEAH.
OLD HABITS DIE HARD, I SUPPOSE.

NO WORRIES. IT'S NICE TO FEEL LIKE SOMEONE STILL CARES ENOUGH TO ASK.

MY PEOPLE WILL BE WATCHING THE AREA, PATROLLING, KEEPING YOU SAFE, BUT IT COULDN'T HURT TO POP YOUR HEAD UP EVERY NOW AND THEN. DON'T GET TOO FOCUSED ON THE DIGGING.
START WITH THE GRASSY AREAS ON EITHER SIDE OF THE ROAD, WE'RE JUST LOOKING FOR A TWO TO THREE FOOT DITCH FOR NOW, SOMETHING TO TRIP THEM UP--WE'RE MAINLY GATHERING UP DIRT UNTIL WE DECIDE IF WE'RE GOING TO DIG UNDER THE PAVEMENT OF THE ROAD OR NOT.
JUST PILE IT UP NEXT TO YOUR HOLE--WE'LL HAVE A GROUP SHOVELING THE PILES INTO THE PICK-UP TRUCK.
LET'S GET STARTED.

WHAT THE HELL ARE WE *DOING?*
DIGGING. I MEAN, RIGHT?

NO, I MEAN-- TAKING ORDERS FROM THESE ASSHOLES. I THINK THINGS WERE JUST FINE BEFORE THEY SHOWED UP.
WHO DIED AND LEFT THEM IN CHARGE?

DOUGLAS DID. OR DID YOU *MISS* THAT PART?

AND YOU KNOW WHAT... THINGS WEREN'T EXACTLY "JUST FINE" BEFORE.
WHAT THE HELL'S WRONG WITH YOU, NICHOLAS?
WATCH IT... YOU KNOW DAMN WELL WE'RE BETTER OFF WITHOUT THESE CRAZY ASSHOLES. YOU FORGET THAT RICK STOLE A GUN AND WAS GOING TO TAKE OVER?!
DON'T YOU GET IT, HEATH? WE JUST HANDED HIM THE KEYS!

SELECTIVE MEMORY, MUCH? RICK WAS DOING THAT TO PROTECT HIS PEOPLE--AND IF HE HADN'T DONE THAT, WE'D HAVE BEEN OVERRUN BY THAT GROUP OF MARAUDERS THAT ATTACKED SHORTLY THEREAFTER.
THESE "CRAZY ASSHOLES" SAVED ALL OUR LIVES.

YOU GOT NO WAY OF KNOWING THAT.
WE COULD HAVE HANDLED THAT.

NO! NO FUCKING WAY COULD WE HAVE GOTTEN THROUGH THAT WITHOUT ANY DEATHS. WE EVER THINK TO PUT SOMEONE IN THAT BELL TOWER ON LOOKOUT? WE HAVE ANYONE GOOD WITH A RIFLE LIKE ANDREA?
WE WERE A NAIVE, SHELTERED BUNCH OF WEAKLINGS... MOST OF US AT LEAST, JUST WAITING TO GET KILLED INSIDE THESE WALLS. WE HAD NO IDEA HOW UNSAFE WE WERE.
THAT'S WHY DOUGLAS PUT RICK IN CHARGE--AND THAT'S WHY I'M GLAD THAT WE'RE TAKING STEPS TO MAKE THIS PLACE SAFER--THINGS WE NEVER WOULD HAVE THOUGHT TO DO.

EVERYTHING OKAY HERE?

YEAH.
WE'RE FINE.

RICK, DO YOU HAVE A MINUTE?
SURE THING...

MAGGIE.
SOPHIA.
AFTERNOON. NOT MUCH OF A SELECTION IN HERE, OLIVIA.

YEAH. THAT'S ACTUALLY WHAT I WANTED TO TALK TO YOU ABOUT, RICK.
WE'RE STARTING TO RUN PRETTY LOW...

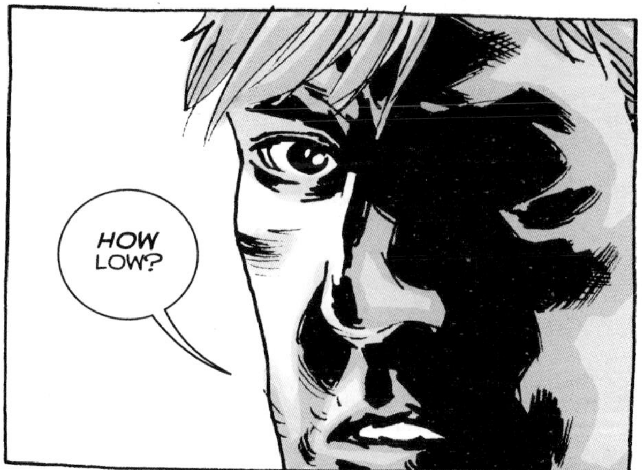
HOW LOW?

WE COULD START TIGHTENING RATIONS, ALTHOUGH I DON'T THINK THAT WOULD GO WELL WITH ALL THIS WORK BEING DONE.
WINTER'S JUST GETTING STARTED... THINGS COULD GET PRETTY BAD HERE IN A FEW WEEKS... AND WE'D BE ALMOST OUT OF FOOD ABOUT THEN.
I THINK WE NEED TO SEND A TEAM OUT, SHORE US UP FOR THE WINTER.

THANKS FOR THE HEADS UP, OLIVIA.
I'LL PUT THAT IN MOTION... SEE IF WE CAN'T SEND PEOPLE OUT TOMORROW.

RICK, WAIT.
WHAT'S THE MATTER?

NOTHING, I'M FINE... LOOK...
DON'T SEND GLENN OUT, OKAY? **PLEASE**. IN FACT... KEEP HIM FROM GOING. HASN'T HE GONE OUT ENOUGH?

HE HAS. AND WE HAVE PEOPLE LIKE HEATH WHO ACTUALLY KNOW THE AREA BETTER.
I'LL MAKE SURE HE DOESN'T GO.

YOU CHECK ON HIM?
STILL ASLEEP. NOTHING YET.
SORRY.

FEEL LIKE I SHOULD BE OUT THERE, IN THE BELL TOWER, KEEPING WATCH.
ABRAHAM AND HIS PEOPLE HAVE IT COVERED-- THEY'RE SAFE OUT THERE.

YOU EVER GET THAT FEELING? OVERWHELMING-- BUT *COMPLETELY* IRRATIONAL CONCERN...
I FEEL LIKE I'M DOING SOMETHING WRONG BY NOT BEING OUT THERE.

CAN'T BE EVERYWHERE. THAT'S A TOUGH LESSON TO LEARN.
BUT YEAH... I FEEL THAT... ALL THE TIME.

ANDREA, GO GET--
RICK, COME INSIDE!

HE JUST STARTED WAKING UP, HE WAS MOVING HIS HEAD AND--
HOLD ON--

CARL, DON'T TOUCH--
STOP MOVING--

IS HE... OKAY?

I DON'T KNOW ANYTHING YET.
I'M SORRY.

...

D-D--

CARL! IT'S ME!
I'M RIGHT HERE! YOU'RE OKAY--YOU'RE SAFE!

...
DAD?

I'M HERE.
IT'S-- IT'S JUST SO GOOD TO HEAR YOUR VOICE.

BE CAREFUL, YOUR WOUND--
WHAT--?

WHAT HAPPENED TO ME?

WHERE'S MOM?

IS MOM HERE?
WHAT HAPPENED?

WHO ARE *YOU?*

I'M DOCTOR DENISE CLOYD, I'M A SURGEON... YOU WERE *SHOT*, CARL. I'VE BEEN WORKING TO...
MAKE YOU BETTER.

SHOT? I WAS...

OH...
OH, GOD...

CARL...

IT'S OKAY.

IT'S GOING TO BE OKAY.

THINGS ARE A LITTLE FUZZY NOW... BUT I'LL EXPLAIN EVERYTHING.
I'LL--

YOU'RE OKAY.
THAT'S ALL THAT MATTERS.

RICK?

HOW IS HE?
HE'S EATING. ANDREA'S WITH HIM.

RICK, HIS COGNITIVE SKILLS SEEM INTACT. I'VE TESTED HIM EXTENSIVELY... AND I SEE NO CAUSE FOR ALARM.
THE MEMORY GAPS... THEY'RE NOT UNCOMMON WITH SEVERE BRAIN TRAUMA. HIS MEMORY COULD COME BACK ON ITS OWN.

WHAT AM I SUPPOSED TO *DO?*

WHAT DO YOU MEAN?
IT SEEMS A HUGE CHUNK OF HIS RECENT MEMORY IS JUST... GONE.
HOW DO I DEAL WITH THAT?

HOW DO I TELL HIM HIS MOTHER IS DEAD?

YEAH.

I CAN'T TELL YOU HOW HAPPY I AM TO HAVE HIM BACK... TO KNOW HE'S ALIVE.
BUT TO GET HIM BACK... ONLY TO HAVE TO TURN AROUND AND BREAK HIS HEART...
...IT CAN NEVER BE EASY... CAN IT?

YOU KNOW WHAT SUCKS...

...THE PHONES AREN'T WORKING. IT'S THE LITTLE THINGS, REALLY, THAT I MISS THE MOST.
SPENCER?!

IF THE PHONES WERE WORKING, I'D HAVE JUST CALLED WHEN WE FINISHED DIGGING OUR HOLES.
INSTEAD, I COME OVER TO TALK, UNANNOUNCED BECAUSE... HOW DO YOU ANNOUNCE YOURSELF NOW ANYWAY?
AND THEN I SEE YOU'RE NOT HERE... RATHER THAN GO LOOKING FOR YOU, WHICH SEEMS CREEPY AND WEIRD... I DECIDE TO WAIT FOR YOU HERE.

BUT THEN I FALL ASLEEP WHILE I'M WAITING... AND HERE I AM, HOURS AFTER DARK, BY THE LOOKS OF IT... ON YOUR PORCH...
...BEING CREEPY.
IF ONLY THE PHONES WORKED.

WHAT DO YOU *WANT?*

I JUST WANTED TO TALK. I KNOW IT'S LATE.
I CAN JUST COME BACK TOMORROW.

I HAVE NOTHING TO SAY TO YOU.

WHY?!
BECAUSE OF ONE COMMENT?! SOMETHING I SAID IN THE HEAT OF THE MOMENT... WHEN OUR LIVES WERE ON THE LINE...
YOU'RE THROUGH WITH ME BECAUSE I THOUGHT ABOUT OUR LIVES OVER THE LIVES OF OTHERS? CAN YOU BLAME ME?!

OH, WAIT...
THAT'S *EXACTLY* WHAT YOU'RE DOING.

SPENCER... LISTEN.
WHATEVER WE HAD, HOWEVER BRIEFLY IT LASTED, I GET THAT IT MEANT A LOT TO YOU.
BUT IT'S *OVER.*

COULD I HAVE READ YOU THAT WRONG? I THOUGHT WE WERE BUILDING SOMETHING...
I THOUGHT WHAT WE HAD WAS SPECIAL.

WE WEREN'T, AND IT WASN'T. OKAY? DONE.
YOU WERE NICE TO ME, I APPRECIATED IT. IN THE END... WE'RE JUST NOT COMPATIBLE.

WHY? WHAT MAKES YOU SAY THAT?
I COULD ARGUE THAT YOU JUST DIDN'T GIVE ME ENOUGH TIME TO SHOW YOU THAT WE'RE COMPATIBLE.

LET ME MAKE THIS AS CLEAR AS I CAN. GET OFF MY FUCKING PORCH.
GO AWAY.

HOW LONG DO I HAVE TO STAY HERE?

DOCTOR CLOYD JUST WANTS TO KEEP AN EYE ON YOU FOR A BIT LONGER.
I'M SURE SHE'LL LET US GO BACK TO OUR HOUSE IN THE MORNING.

THAT'S RIGHT... WE LIVE IN A HOUSE NOW. I'M... STARTING TO REMEMBER.
IS MOM THERE?

CARL...
YOUR MOTHER DIED...

OH...

HOW DID SHE DIE?

SHE WAS CARRYING JUDY... THEY WERE BOTH SHOT.

WHO'S JUDY?

SHE WAS YOUR SISTER...
...SHE WAS...
...JUST A BABY...

MY SISTER...
...I DON'T REMEMBER HER.

CARL?

YEAH?

ARE YOU SAD?

I DON'T THINK SO.
I MISS MOM, BUT EVEN THOUGH I DON'T REMEMBER... IT DOESN'T FEEL LIKE SHE'S ALIVE. SHE FEELS... **GONE.**
I DON'T REMEMBER JUDY. IT'S SAD THAT SHE'S DEAD... BUT MOST EVERYONE I KNOW IS DEAD. I REMEMBER AMY DIED. I LIKED HER. AND SOPHIA'S MOM DIED. TYREESE DIED. MORGAN DIED, AND...
...JESSIE AND RON DIED, TOO...

YOU REMEMBER JESSIE AND RON?

I KNOW THEY'RE DEAD. I THINK THEY WERE ATTACKED. WAS I THERE?

YOU WERE, YES.
I'M TIRED NOW, CAN I GO TO SLEEP?

YES.

HOLY FUCK, I JUST HEARD THE NEWS. THE KID WOKE UP?!
YEAH... BUT HE'S ASLEEP. ONLY JUST NOW, TOO. I HAVEN'T SLEPT ALL NIGHT.

WELL, BY GOD, GO GET SOME DAMN SLEEP.
I CAN'T. OLIVIA TOLD ME YESTERDAY THAT FOOD IS STARTING TO RUN LOW--WE NEED TO SEND A GROUP OUT TO SEARCH FOR SUPPLIES.
CAN YOU GATHER UP SOME PEOPLE? KIND OF IMPORTANT WE DO IT TODAY, I THINK.

WE'RE NOT GOING TO FUCKING RUN OUT OF FOOD *TODAY*. WE MAKE A RUN TOMORROW-- OR WE SEND GLENN AND HEATH, WHY DO YOU NEED TO BE UP?

CAN'T SEND GLENN.
AND I WANT TO GO OUT, MYSELF.

WHY NOT AND WHY THE FUCK?

BECAUSE MAGGIE ASKED ME NOT TO. GLENN ALWAYS GOES, IT'S ALWAYS KIND OF BEEN HIS THING.
SHE THINKS IT'S NOT FAIR AND SHE'S RIGHT.

I WANT TO GO BECAUSE I WANT TO REALLY SEARCH THE AREA AROUND US. THERE ARE SHOPS AND RESIDENCES ALL AROUND US. I WANT TO STAY CLOSE AND MAKE SURE WE'VE EXHAUSTED ALL THE RESOURCES NEAR US.
I WANT TO DO THINGS DIFFERENTLY. NOT A SMALL, FAST GROUP LIKE USUAL--BUT A LARGE, SAFE, SECURE GROUP--THAT CAN SCOUR THE AREA TOGETHER, WATCH EACH OTHER'S BACKS.
WE WON'T NEED TO TAKE A VEHICLE, WE'LL JUST SPEND THE DAY SEARCHING A FEW BLOCKS AROUND US.

IT NEEDS TO BE TODAY, JUST IN CASE THIS TRIP YIELDS NOTHING. I DON'T WANT TO PUSH THINGS OFF. I WANT TO KNOW IF WE NEED TO KEEP SEARCHING FURTHER AWAY.
AND I'M GOING BECAUSE CARL'S SLEEPING, AND I CAN'T... AND HE'S NOT... HE'S FORGOTTEN THINGS, ABRAHAM. LOTS OF THINGS... AND I CAN'T DEAL WITH IT RIGHT NOW.
I NEED THE DISTRACTION.

OKAY.
UNDERSTOOD.

HOW IS HE?
STILL SLEEPING.

I'M GOING TO GO OUT--WE NEED TO SEARCH FOR FOOD. CAN YOU, KEEP AN EYE ON HIM?

HE JUST WOKE UP FROM A COMA, RICK. HE WON'T SLEEP VERY LONG.
WHY ARE *YOU* GOING?

I HAVE-- I NEED TO...
JUST WATCH CARL FOR ME, OKAY?

HE'S YOUR SON. HE'S GOING TO WAKE UP SCARED... ALONE.
WHY WOULD YOU DO THIS?

...

JUST TAKE CARE OF HIM.

ABRAHAM SAYS YOU'RE GOING OUT AND I'M NOT ALLOWED TO COME?
WHAT'S THAT ABOUT?

IT'S FOR MAGGIE. SHE BEGGED ME NOT TO SEND YOU.
I'M NOT SAYING YOU CAN'T GO OUT, I JUST THOUGHT, FOR HER, MIGHT AS WELL LET YOU SIT ONE OUT.

FEELS LIKE I'M SLACKING OFF OR SOMETHING, BUT SURE.
FOR MAGGIE. SHE HAD A HARD TIME WITH ME ON THE OTHER SIDE OF THAT WALL LAST TIME. I GET IT.

ALSO, WE'RE DOING THINGS A LITTLE DIFFERENTLY. I'M NOT SENDING A COUPLE PEOPLE OUT-- WE'RE GOING OUT AS A BIG GROUP.
SO I'D FEEL A LOT BETTER IF YOU KEPT AN EYE ON THINGS WHILE I WAS GONE.
YEAH, OKAY. I'LL... DO A PATROL OR SOMETHING.
OKAY.

WE'RE ALL AT THE GATE, READY WHEN YOU ARE.

THANKS, GLENN.

READY?
YEAH. LET'S FUCK THIS DOG.

NICE.
LOVE YA.

SO YOU JUST WANT TO CHECK THE STREETS AROUND HERE FOR THINGS? I'M PRETTY SURE WE'RE NOT GOING TO FIND MUCH.
AARON AND I SPENT A LOT OF TIME CHECKING THE AREA EARLY ON.

OUR GOALS TODAY ARE TWO-FOLD. I WANT TO FIND FOOD, BUT I ALSO WOULD LIKE TO SPEND SOME TIME MAPPING OUT THE AREA AROUND US.
I'D LIKE TO GET A FEEL FOR WHAT WE HAVE IN OUR BACKYARD, SEE IF THERE'S ANYTHING WE CAN USE.
IF WE DON'T FIND ANY FOOD TODAY--WE'LL EXPAND OUR SEARCH TOMORROW.

WE'RE WASTING DAYLIGHT--LET'S GO.

BE CAREFUL OUT THERE!

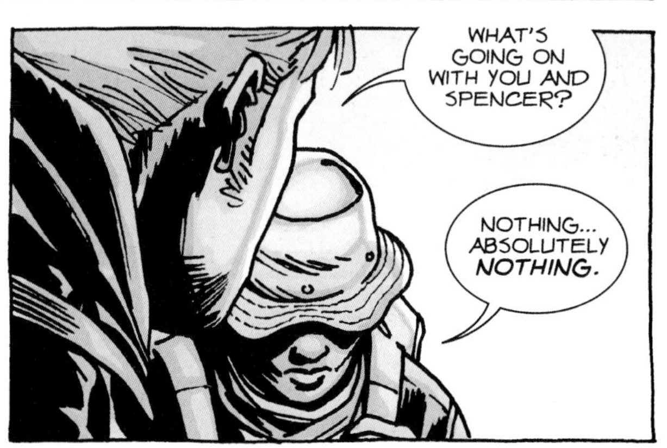
WHAT'S GOING ON WITH YOU AND SPENCER?
NOTHING... ABSOLUTELY *NOTHING.*

I GOT IT.

NOT MANY AROUND LAST COUPLE DAYS, HUH?

IT'S BEEN COLD ENOUGH RECENTLY, DAMN THINGS ARE PROBABLY MOSTLY FROZEN.
WE RAN INTO THAT A LOT LAST WINTER.

WRAKK!

LET'S CHECK OUT THESE STORES. REMEMBER--GENERAL SUPPLIES, FOOD, THAT KIND OF THING.
STAY WITHIN SHOUTING DISTANCE OF EACH OTHER--AND STAY ALERT.

YEAH, KEEP YOUR EARS OPEN, PEOPLE.
THESE FUCKERS ARE SLOWER--BUT STILL DANGEROUS.

STALE POTATO CHIPS-- SCORE!

ANYTHING?
NOTHING.

RICK!

RICK?
OFFICE
PRIVATE

...

WHAT'S WRONG?

THEY HAVE SOME SPECIFIC PLACE PICKED OUT FOR THIS DIRT?
JUST PACK IT AGAINST THE BACK OF THE FENCE IS ALL THEY SAID. MIGHT AS WELL START NEXT TO THE GATE, RIGHT?

CAN I HELP?

YEAH, COME HERE.

REAL QUICK, WHILE WE'RE ALONE...
I TALKED TO HEATH YESTERDAY, AND HE'S FURTHER UP RICK'S ASS THAN I THOUGHT.
WAS TALKING ABOUT HOW WE NEED HIM TO PROTECT US AND ALL KINDS OF SHIT.

SO WHAT ARE YOU SAYING, NICHOLAS?

I'M SAYING THAT IF WE'RE GOING TO MAKE A MOVE, WE NEED TO DO IT SOON BEFORE HE WINS OVER *EVERYONE*.

WE LEAVE THESE CRAZY ASSHOLES IN CHARGE LONG ENOUGH--AND THEY'LL BE THE DEATH OF US *ALL*.

IF I'M HONEST... I DON'T KNOW THAT I NECESSARILY AGREE WITH THAT.
DON'T GET ME WRONG, I'M WITH YOU... RICK SHOULDN'T BE IN CHARGE. IT'S WEIRD THAT HE'S SUDDENLY RUNNING THINGS.
BUT I DON'T THINK HE'LL GET US ALL KILLED.

WHAT?! SERIOUSLY?!
WHERE IS EVERYONE, OLIVIA? OUT COMBING THROUGH BUILDINGS THAT WERE SEARCHED LONG AGO?
WHAT ABOUT HAVING US DIG A TRENCH AROUND THIS PLACE--OUT IN THE OPEN--EXPOSED? THAT SEEM SAFE?

AND YOU'VE SEEN THIS GUY IN ACTION. WHAT IS IT YOU THINK HE'D DO, WERE WE TO REFUSE HIS BULLSHIT TASKS?
YOU THINK HE'D UNDERSTAND, ASSIGN US TO SOMETHING ELSE?
OR YOU THINK WE'D BE TAKING ORDERS DOWN THE BARREL OF A GUN?

SO OUR OPTIONS ARE CLEAR.
WE KILL RICK BEFORE HE KILLS US.

DAMN. UH...
I WASN'T HERE... I DIDN'T--

IT WASN'T SUPPOSED TO GO DOWN LIKE THIS...

RICK?
ARE YOU OKAY?

YEAH, IT'S NOTHING.
JUST A LITTLE... WELL... I'M CLEARLY UPSET.
SORRY.

ALL YOU'VE DONE FOR ME? NOT MUCH NEED TO APOLOGIZE FOR ANYTHING.

EVERYONE LOOKS TO ME FOR LEADERSHIP... I'M SUPPOSED TO BE THE STRONG ONE.
I HATE FOR ***ANYONE*** TO SEE ME LIKE THIS.

ALL THIS TIME, WHAT WE'VE BEEN THROUGH, TOGETHER... IT'S OKAY.
OKAY?
ANYTHING I CAN DO TO HELP?

NO, IT'S ***NOTHING.***
MY DAD ALWAYS GAVE ME THE WHOLE "BOYS DON'T CRY" SPEECH. I TRIED ALL I COULD TO ADHERE TO THAT... JUST NEVER REALLY WORKED OUT THAT WAY.
FEEL LIKE I'VE ALWAYS BEEN A FEW THOUGHTS FROM CRYING... ALL MY LIFE. MORE SO NOW, WITH EVERYTHING...

SCHOOL YARD FIGHTS NEVER WENT SO WELL FOR ME--THAT ADRENALINE RUSH ALWAYS GOT THE TEARS FLOWING... MADE IT HARD TO LOOK TOUGH.
I GOT A BETTER HANDLE ON IT WHEN I WAS OLDER... BUT NOW, IT'S JUST...
THERE'S AN AWFUL LOT WORTH CRYING ABOUT THESE DAYS.
YEAH...

BUT THAT WHOLE LEADER THING... IT'S KIND OF TRUE, AND AS MUCH AS I LIKE-- HELL, I'VE GROWN TO LOVE YOU--I REALLY DON'T WANT TO WALK OUT OF HERE THINKING YOU'RE SOME OVERLY EMOTIONAL MESS THAT'S BREAKING INTO TEARS AT A MOMENT'S NOTICE.
SO HOW ABOUT YOU TELL ME WHAT'S REALLY GOING ON?

...

IT'S CARL...

I CAN'T IMAGINE WHAT YOU'RE GOING THROUGH RIGHT NOW... HE'S YOUR SON, I UNDERSTAND HOW PAINFUL THIS MUST HAVE BEEN... BUT HE'S GOING TO GET HIS MEMORY BACK.
HE'S ALIVE AND--
IT'S NOT THAT...

HE REMEMBERS SOME THINGS, SOME THINGS HE DOESN'T. I'VE REMINDED HIM OF OTHER THINGS...
HE KNOWS HIS MOTHER IS DEAD... AND HE DOESN'T *MISS* HER. HE'S MOVED ON.
IT'S LIKE HE'S TOO STRONG TO GRIEVE... AND GOD HELP ME...

...I'M STARTING TO *HATE* HIM FOR IT.

RICK, HE--
HE'S JUST A BOY...

I *KNOW*...

NO, HE'S--HE'S *FAKING* IT. HE'S TRYING TO LOOK STRONG, FOR YOU--BECAUSE HE SEES *YOU* BEING SO STRONG.
HE WANTS YOUR APPROVAL. HE WANTS YOU TO BE *PROUD* OF HIM...

NO. THAT'S WHAT I USED TO THINK... WHAT I STILL WANT TO THINK...
BUT I CAN'T.
AFTER EVERYTHING HE'S SEEN... EVERYTHING HE'S DONE. MY SON... MY GOD, HE'S BEEN CHANGED SO MUCH.

IT'S NOT HIS FAULT, THAT'S WHAT I KEEP TELLING MYSELF. HE'S HAD TO DO THIS... ADAPT. THAT'S THE ONLY WAY HE SURVIVES.
WHEN WE GOT HERE, I THOUGHT BEING HERE, BEHIND THE WALLS... SAFE... WOULD BRING HIM BACK TO... HOW HE USED TO BE.
I EXPECTED... I DON'T KNOW...

I EXPECTED IT ALL TO JUST WASH AWAY, I SUPPOSE. THE PAIN HE'S LIVED THROUGH... THE HORRORS HE'S SEEN...
I EXPECTED TO SEE THAT SPARKLE IN HIS EYE AGAIN... THAT... HOPE...

INSTEAD, THINGS HAVE JUST GOTTEN WORSE.
UNTIL NOW... NOW I FEEL LIKE WE FINALLY HAVE A CHANCE TO FIX THINGS... WE'RE SO CLOSE TO HAVING THINGS ALMOST LIKE THEY WERE BEFORE ALL THIS STARTED... BUT CARL--HE'S... TOO FAR GONE.

ANDREA...
WHAT GOOD IS KEEPING HIM ALIVE... IF I'VE LOST MY LITTLE BOY IN THE PROCESS?

GUYS, LISTEN. LET'S NOT DO ANYTHING CRAZY, OKAY?
WE'RE ALL IN THIS TOGETHER. JUST BECAUSE RICK AND THE REST OF US CAME LATER-- DOESN'T MEAN WE HAVE TO BE OUTSIDERS.
YOU DON'T HAVE TO DO THIS.

YOU DON'T KNOW WHAT THE FUCK YOU'RE TALKING ABOUT.

HOW MANY OF US HAVE YOUR PEOPLE GOTTEN KILLED?!
WE'RE DROPPING LIKE FLIES OUT HERE--AND THINGS ARE JUST GETTING WORSE!
YOU EXPECT US TO DO NOTHING?!
NICHOLAS, PLEASE...

...IT DOESN'T HAVE TO BE LIKE THIS.

WRAMM!
HAVE YOU LOST YOUR MIND?!

YOU PULL A GUN--?!
KRAK!

--ON ME?!
WROK!

STOP! THAT'S TOO MUCH!
HE WAS JUST SCARED!

BACK OFF!

HE SHOULD BE SCARED.
THEY ALL SHOULD.

PULL A FUCKING GUN ON ME?

HOW DOES IT FEEL?

WELL?!

WRAMM!

FUCK.

WE SHOULD BE HEADING BACK, START GATHERING EVERYONE.
KEEP IT QUIET, I THINK WE'VE BEEN LUCKY SO FAR.
YEAH.

FIND SOMETHING?
NOTHING TO BRAG ABOUT. SOME CANNED CORN--A BAG OF CHIPS THAT I'M PROBABLY THE ONLY ONE BRAVE ENOUGH TO EAT.
IT'S LIKE I SAID, THIS AREA'S BEEN PRETTY MUCH PICKED CLEAN.

I GET THAT, AARON. STILL, IT'S GOOD TO GET A LOOK AT THESE STREETS.
I'M THINKING NOW THAT THE MOAT AND WHATEVER BARRIERS WE PUT AROUND US CAN BE A LAST LINE OF DEFENSE. SOME OF THESE STREETS ARE SO NARROW IT'LL ONLY TAKE THREE CARS TO COMPLETELY BLOCK ANY ROAMERS GETTING THROUGH.

MAKES ME WONDER WHY YOU GUYS HAVEN'T DONE THAT BEFORE.
ERIC AND I WERE THE ONLY ONES TO SPEND A LOT OF TIME OUTSIDE. IF IT CAME UP, I CAN ONLY GUESS DOUGLAS OR TOBIN THOUGHT IT'D BE TOO DANGEROUS TO BE OUTSIDE THE WALLS MAKING THAT MUCH NOISE.
WELL, WE'VE BEEN FINE.
AS LONG AS WE'RE QUIET, THIS AREA SEEMS PRETTY SAFE.

OKAY...
SPOKE TOO SOON.

ABRAHAM, YOU GOT THAT ONE?

WHUKK!
YEP.

THUKK!

WRAMM!
THERE YOU ARE. HAD NO IDEA WHERE YOU'D GONE.

WAS IN THE JEWELRY SHOP. DIDN'T FIND FUCK ALL.
YOU GUYS HAVE ANY LUCK?

CHECKED A FEW APARTMENTS-- KILLED A WALKER, NOTHING OF NOTE.

I FOUND A BUNCH OF CLOTHES, COULD BE USEFUL TO US-- BUT IT'S TOO MUCH TO CARRY, WE'D NEED TO SEND A COUPLE PEOPLE BACK HERE WITH THE TRUCK.
WE CAN DO THAT. SOUNDS LIKE WE'VE CONFIRMED THIS AREA HAS BEEN CLEANED OUT. WE'RE GOING TO NEED TO EXPAND OUR SEARCH.
MIGHT AS WELL HEAD BACK IN.

MAGGIE! YOUR GUN!
GET SOPHIA!

GLENN-- WHAT HAPPENED?!

JUST GIVE ME YOUR GUN, TAKE SOPHIA UPSTAIRS AND LOCK YOURSELF IN THE BATHROOM!
NOW!
WHAT HAPPENED?
NO TIME, PLEASE-- JUST GO.

YOU THINK YOU'RE SAFE IN THERE?!
NICHOLAS, DAMN IT-- HOW FAR ARE YOU GOING TO TAKE THIS?

MIGHT AS WELL GET STARTED--EVERYONE WILL RALLY BEHIND US ONCE WE KICK INTO GEAR. WE OUT-NUMBER THESE PEOPLE.
THERE'S NO TURNING BACK NOW, THE BOY KNOWS WHAT WE WERE PLANNING.
YEAH, BUT-- I DIDN'T THINK THIS IS HOW IT WOULD GO DOWN.

WHAT THE HELL IS GOING ON?!

NONE OF YOUR GODDAMN BUSINESS, TRAITOR.

NICHOLAS, HAVE YOU LOST YOUR GODDAMN MIND?!

LOST MY--?!
I'M THE ONLY ONE WHO'S THINKING CLEARLY AROUND HERE!!

AM I THE ONLY ONE WHO'S NOTICED WE'VE BEEN OVERRUN-- TAKEN OVER BY CRAZY PEOPLE?!
WE USED TO BE SAFE! WE USED TO BE HAPPY! NOW RICK HAS US RUNNING OUTSIDE, DIGGING HOLES AND SEARCHING PLACES WE'VE ALREADY SEARCHED!

DOESN'T THIS SEEM SUSPICIOUS?! I THINK HE WANTS THIS PLACE FOR HIMSELF--I THINK HE'S TRYING TO PICK US OFF--ONE BY ONE!
NOBODY PUT HIM IN CHARGE--HE CAME HERE--AND JUST TOOK OVER!
I CAN'T BE THE ONLY ONE WHO'S NOTICED THIS!

NOW THIS LITTLE FUCKER INSIDE IS GOING TO TELL RICK WE'RE ONTO HIM. WE NEED TO TAKE HIM OUT BEFORE RICK RETURNS!
NOT LIKE THIS, MAN.

YOU BETTER MAN UP AND BACK MY PLAY HERE! THIS IS YOUR FATHER'S LEGACY AT STAKE.
THIS IS NO TIME FOR COLD GODDAMN FEET.

GLENN!
GET OUT HERE BEFORE I COME IN THERE AND KIL EVERY DAMN ONE OF YOU INSIDE!

PUT THE GUN DOWN NOW!

GET BACK!
EVERYONE, STAY BACK! IF YOU'RE NOT WITH ME, YOU'RE WITH THEM!

GET AWAY FROM MY HOUSE-- AND STOP THREATENING MY FAMILY!

WE ALL KNOW WHO THE REAL THREAT IS!

WHAT THE HELL IS GOING ON HERE?!

ANSWERS-- NOW!

I'M--I'M TAKING THIS PLACE BACK.

FROM ANDREA?

FROM ABRAHAM?

YOU'RE TAKING THE COMMUNITY BACK?
REALLY?

FROM MICHONNE?

FROM GLENN?

FROM ME?
DO YOU HAVE ANY FUCKING IDEA WHO YOU'RE TALKING TO?

PUT.
THE GUN.
DOWN.

OKAY...

...WHAT DO WE DO NOW?

WHAT'S THE SAYING... OH, YEAH... "UNITED WE STAND, DIVIDED WE FALL," RIGHT? IT WAS ON THE BACK OF THE DOLLAR, FOR CHRIST'S SAKE.
OF COURSE-- IT'S BEEN A WHILE SINCE I LOOKED.
SO, DO I HAVE TO SAY ANYTHING ELSE? CAN I JUST LEAVE IT AT THAT? BECAUSE I'M TIRED AND I HAVE MUCH BETTER THINGS TO DO.

YOU'RE NOT...
...GOING TO KILL US?

YOU THINK WE WANT TO KILL YOU?

YOU'RE STUPIDER THAN I THOUGHT.

YOU PEOPLE HAVE NO IDEA WHAT YOU HAVE HERE. YOU HAVEN'T BEEN THROUGH WHAT WE'VE BEEN THROUGH, SEEN WHAT WE'VE SEEN.
WHAT YOU'VE GOT HERE PASSES FOR PARADISE THESE DAYS.
CLOSEST WE GOT TO THIS BEFORE WAS A COLD, HARD PRISON... BUT THE MOST IMPORTANT THING YOU HAVE HERE, SOMETHING I'D NEVER REALIZED UNTIL RECENTLY...
...IS PEOPLE.

SO NO, WE DON'T WANT TO KILL YOU, NICHOLAS. YOU'RE A FATHER, A GOOD MAN-- AND I THINK WE CAN PUT THIS MATTER TO BED ONCE AND FOR ALL.
WE NEED YOU.

BUT MORE IMPORTANTLY FOR YOU-- YOU NEED US.

...BY WORKING TOGETHER.
THAT'S HOW WE SURVIVE. THAT'S HOW IT WILL BE POSSIBLE FOR US TO MAKE A LIFE HERE, LONG TERM...

UNITED WE STAND... AND ALL THE REST.
GET IT?

Y--YEAH.

DON'T THINK WE WON'T BE KEEPING AN EYE ON YOU NOW. NOT BECAUSE WE'RE OUT TO GET YOU--BUT TO ENSURE THE SAFETY OF ALL OF US.
SO YOU BETTER MIND YOUR MANNERS... AND IF YOU EVER HAVE AN ISSUE WITH US--YOU COME TO US BEFORE YOU LET IT DRIVE YOU CRAZY AGAIN.
GOT IT?

YES.

GOOD.

GO *HOME*.

GOOD JOB.
...
THANKS.

DOCTOR CLOYD-- WAIT!

HAS CARL WOKEN UP?
NO, NOT LAST I LOOKED-- DON'T KNOW HOW HE COULD HAVE SLEPT THROUGH THIS, THOUGH.

WHAT HAPPENED?
I HEARD A LOT OF YELLING OUTSIDE.

IT WAS NOTHING. SOME OF THE PEOPLE HERE WERE CAUSING A LITTLE TROUBLE, BUT IT'S ALL UNDER CONTROL NOW.

DID YOU HAVE TO KILL ANYBODY?

NO. I DIDN'T.
DOCTOR CLOYD SAID YOU COULD COME *HOME* IF YOU'D LIKE.
WHAT DO YOU THINK?

HOW DO YOU FEEL?
NOT GOOD... BUT OKAY. I'M HUNGRY.
I'LL GET YOU SOMETHING AS SOON AS WE GET HOME.

I WAS REALLY WORRIED ABOUT YOU, CARL.

DAD, IF I HAD DIED...

WOULD YOU HAVE BEEN SAD?

CARL...
...WHY WOULD YOU ASK ME THAT?

BECAUSE YOU'RE SO STRONG...
...I MEAN, I KNOW YOU LOVE ME, DAD... BUT... YOU WOULDN'T BE...
...RIGHT?

CARL, IF ANYTHING WERE TO HAPPEN TO YOU, IF I LOST YOU--I'D BE DEVASTATED AND THAT HAS NOTHING TO DO WITH HOW STRONG I AM.
IT DOESN'T?
NO, IT'S... THAT'S NOT HOW THINGS WORK AND...

BUT I THOUGHT YOU HAD TO NOT BE SAD, I REMEMBER THAT... I REMEMBER HAVING TO NOT BE SAD AFTER MOM DIED. NOW...
I'M STARTING TO REMEMBER THINGS.
I'M STRONG, AREN'T I?

YES, BUT... BEING SAD ISN'T A WEAKNESS--IT'S A FACT OF LIFE, IT'S NOT REALLY SOMETHING YOU CAN CONTROL.
YOU... MISS YOUR MOM, CARL. IT'S VERY SAD THAT SHE'S GONE... AND WHILE YOU MAY NOT WANT TO SHOW IT--YOU CAN'T DENY IT... IT'S THERE.

YEAH.

I NEED YOU TO DO SOMETHING FOR ME, CARL. I NEED YOU TO LET IT ALL GO.
WHAT?

I NEED YOU TO STOP BEING SO DAMN STRONG... I NEED YOU TO LET YOURSELF BE SCARED, AND LET YOURSELF FEEL, AND BE HAPPY, AND... I NEED YOU TO PRETEND THINGS CAN BE LIKE THEY WERE...
BEFORE ALL THIS...

I DON'T UNDERSTAND.

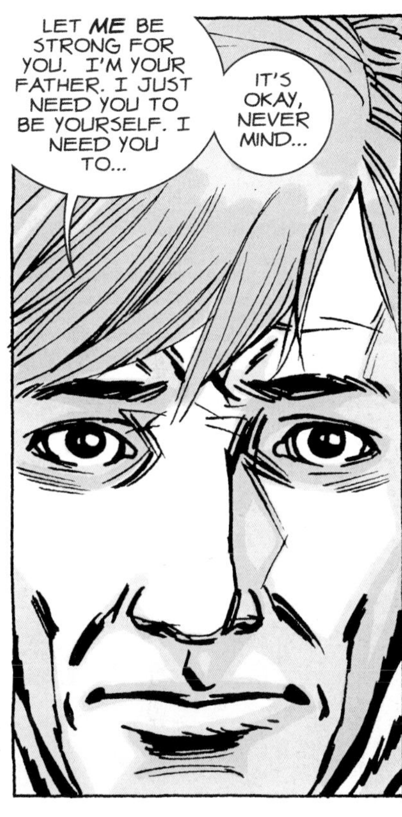
LET ME BE STRONG FOR YOU. I'M YOUR FATHER. I JUST NEED YOU TO BE YOURSELF. I NEED YOU TO...
IT'S OKAY, NEVER MIND...

COME HERE.

I HAVE A WIFE AND A KID...
CARL, GO INSIDE.

I SAW THEM, AND I WAS SO GRATEFUL TO YOU-- THAT I GOT TO SEE THEM AGAIN, AFTER I WENT HOME.
AND, IT MADE ME... HOW CLOSE I CAME MADE ME REALIZE, JUST HOW THAT... ALL OF THAT, MY GOD, IT WAS DRIVEN BY EGO.

COME AGAIN?
I DON'T WANT TO BE YOUR DITCH DIGGER. I WAS A FAILURE IN THE WORLD BEFORE... I... AFTER A WHILE, I WAS LUCKY TO GET A JOB DIGGING DITCHES.

AND THIS... WHAT'S HAPPENED TO ALL OF US, THIS WAS SUPPOSED TO BE AN OPPORTUNITY TO DO BETTER, TO MAKE SOMETHING BETTER OF MYSELF... AND I FELT LIKE YOU WERE KEEPING ME FROM THAT.
BUT IT WAS ME. IT'S ALWAYS BEEN ME.
OKAY...
WHAT NOW THEN?

THERE'S NO RULE BOOK. THAT, I THINK... THAT'S WHAT I'M HERE TO SAY.
GOD, I SOUND LIKE AN *IDIOT.*
I JUST MEAN, IT'S *EASY* TO BECOME IRRATIONAL. EVEN IF THAT'S... NOT A NORMAL THING FOR YOU, AND...

IT'S HARD, YOU KNOW THAT-- BUT EVEN IN HERE, BEHIND THESE WALLS, IT'S NOT EASY... LIVING.
I HAVE TO WORRY ABOUT MY WIFE AND SON, I HAVE TO KEEP THEM HAPPY... HELL, MY BOY DOESN'T **KNOW** HALF OF WHAT'S GOING ON. WHEN THE WALKERS STARTED COMING THROUGH THE WALL... THAT'S THE FIRST DANGER HE'S KNOWN.

WHAT I'M GETTING AT... IS I KIND OF LOST IT. I DIDN'T SEE YOU FOR WHO YOU WERE AND I WAS SCARED, DESPERATE.
YOU HAD ME DEAD TO RIGHTS, AND HAD EVERY REASON IN THE WORLD TO TAKE ME OUT--I REALIZE THAT NOW.
AND YOU DIDN'T... FOR THAT, I THANK YOU.
AND I GET THAT YOU'RE GOING TO KEEP AN EYE ON ME, I UNDERSTAND WHY. BUT I WANT TO REASSURE YOU.

I'M NOT CRAZY... I'M NOT DANGEROUS. THINGS JUST... GOT TO ME...
I'M QUICK-TEMPERED, THAT'S TRUE-- BUT THINGS JUST... I LOST MYSELF.
BUT HEARING YOU TALK... IT'S BROUGHT ME BACK, MADE ME FEEL OPTIMISTIC AGAIN, LIKE THINGS ACTUALLY ***COULD*** GET BETTER.
I... LOOK, AS A FAMILY MAN-- I'M ***WITH*** YOU. OKAY?
YEAH, THANKS.

OKAY, THEN. I'LL LEAVE YOU TO BE WITH YOUR SON.
ALL RIGHT. GOOD NIGHT, THEN.

WHAT WAS THAT ALL ABOUT?

CHRIST...

WHAT?

I DON'T EVEN KNOW WHERE TO BEGIN...
...THIS WAS ALL ONE DAY?

SO... WE'RE RUNNING LOW ON FOOD.
YEAH.

AND MY FELLOW ORIGINAL COMMUNITY MEMBERS ARE LOSING THEIR MINDS.
SEEMS THAT WAY.

AND WE'RE WORKING OUR ASSES OFF TO SECURE AND PROTECT THIS POWDER KEG THAT COULD BLOW AT ANY MINUTE.
YOU COULD SAY THAT.

IT SEEMS TO ME...

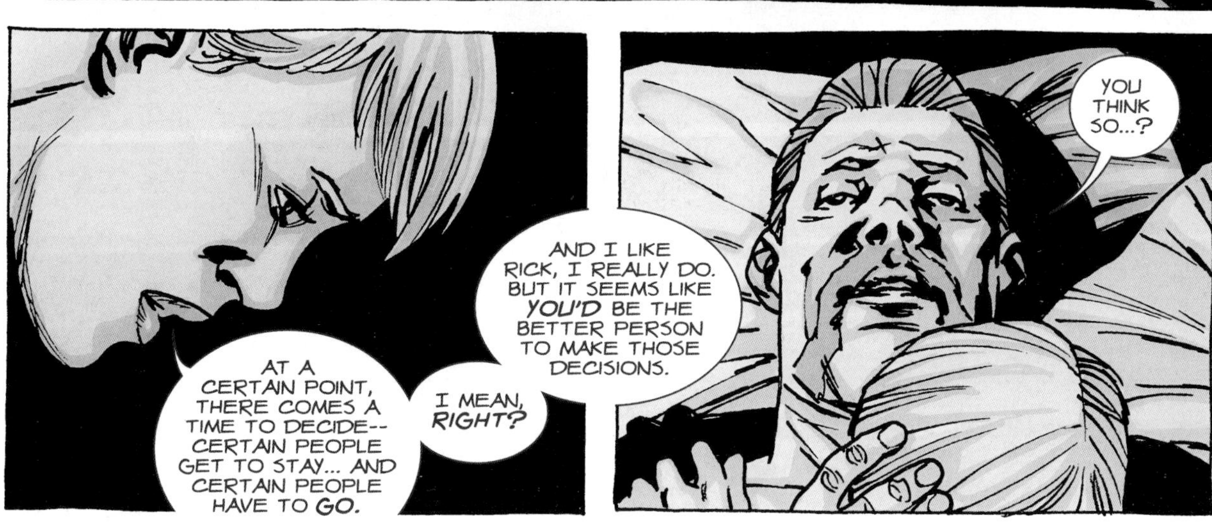
AT A CERTAIN POINT, THERE COMES A TIME TO DECIDE-- CERTAIN PEOPLE GET TO STAY... AND CERTAIN PEOPLE HAVE TO GO.
YOU THINK SO...?
I MEAN, RIGHT?
AND I LIKE RICK, I REALLY DO. BUT IT SEEMS LIKE YOU'D BE THE BETTER PERSON TO MAKE THOSE DECISIONS.

GOODNIGHT, SOPHIA. WE'LL SEE YOU IN MORNING.
WHY ARE WE EVEN PRETENDING? THERE'S NO *WAY* SHE'S GOING TO SLEEP AFTER ALL THAT.

SHH... ESPECIALLY NOT AFTER HEARING YOU SAY *THAT.*
SORRY.

IT'S JUST... I KNOW I'M NOT GOING TO BE SLEEPING. THAT CRAZY ASSHOLE POINTED A GUN AT ME--BEAT ME UP...
AND NOW HE'S OUT THERE, UNCHECKED. I MEAN, I'M SURE RICK'S GOT SOMEONE KEEPING AN EYE ON HIM. I THINK MICHONNE STILL DOES NIGHT PATROLS... BUT STILL.

WHAT'S WRONG?

I CAN'T DO THIS ANYMORE...
I JUST CAN'T...

I WANT TO FEEL SAFE AGAIN. I JUST... WHY CAN'T I FEEL SAFE?
WITH YOU GOING OUT--ON THE OTHER SIDE OF THE WALL WHEN THAT HERD CAME THROUGH--BLOCKING US IN HERE--I NEARLY LOST MY MIND.
I ASKED RICK NOT TO TAKE YOU... TO LEAVE YOU HERE, SO YOU'D BE... SAFE...

MAGGIE, COME ON...

NO, I THOUGHT WE WERE SAFE HERE, BEHIND THE WALLS, IN THESE HOUSES.
BUT WE'RE NOT.

I JUST....
WE WERE LIVING LIKE THAT, FOR SO LONG, NO SECURITY, LIVING AT RISK...

I CAN'T GO BACK TO THAT. NOT NOW.
I CAN'T LIVE LIKE THIS.

CARL?
READING. I DON'T THINK *EITHER* OF US WILL SLEEP MUCH TONIGHT.

HE'S GOING TO BE OKAY, ISN'T HE?

YEAH, I THINK HE WILL BE.
I MEAN, AS MUCH AS *ANY* OF US WILL BE.

ANDREA, I NEED TO TELL SOMEONE... I... I WANTED TO *KILL* HIM.
THAT MAN TODAY-- NICHOLAS.

HE HAD A GUN POINTED AT GLENN, OF COURSE YOU DID.
I WAS THERE. I KNOW WHAT HE TRIED TO DO.

NO, YOU DON'T GET IT. I DIDN'T *NEED* TO, I *WANTED* TO KILL HIM-- I EVEN THOUGHT, WHEN I WAS TALKING TO HIM, HOW MUCH EASIER IT'D BE IF I JUST KILLED HIM, RIGHT THEN AND THERE.
I WANTED TO KILL HIM BECAUSE OF HOW *PATHETIC* HE IS... LIKE HE HOLDS NO VALUE.
I'VE DONE IT SO MANY TIMES, IT'S... IT'S SOMETHING I *CASUALLY* THINK ABOUT WHEN SOMEONE COMES INTO CONFLICT WITH ME, KILLING THEM.
THAT'S FUCKED UP-- I MEAN... THAT'S *TERRIFYING*... RIGHT?

HERE I AM, TRYING TO GET CARL TO OPEN UP, HAVE FEELINGS AGAIN, LIVE HIS LIFE... BE A KID.
HOW CAN I EXPECT THAT FROM HIM WHEN I CAN BARELY LOOK AT A MAN WITHOUT WANTING TO BLOW HIS HEAD OFF?
COME ON, THAT'S NOT TRUE.

NO, LISTEN... I'VE BEEN TRYING TO CHANGE THINGS, HOW PEOPLE THINK, HOW THEY ACT-- GET US TO WORK TOGETHER, TO BUILD A BETTER, SAFER PLACE TO LIVE...
...TO BUILD A BETTER LIFE FOR ALL OF US.

YEAH?

IT'S A LIFE I DON'T EVEN THINK I'M CAPABLE OF LIVING ANYMORE... I JUST DON'T FIT INTO A SAFE WORLD.

NONSENSE.
NO, LOOK AT ME... REALLY, JUST... LOOK INTO MY EYES...

...CAN'T YOU SEE IT?
THERE'S NOTHING LEFT IN ME, NOT ANYMORE. I FEEL LIKE I DIED A LONG TIME AGO.

HAVE YOU FORGOTTEN? DEATH DOESN'T AFFECT PEOPLE QUITE LIKE IT USED TO.
DON'T YOU THINK IT'S ABOUT TIME YOU CAME BACK TO LIFE?

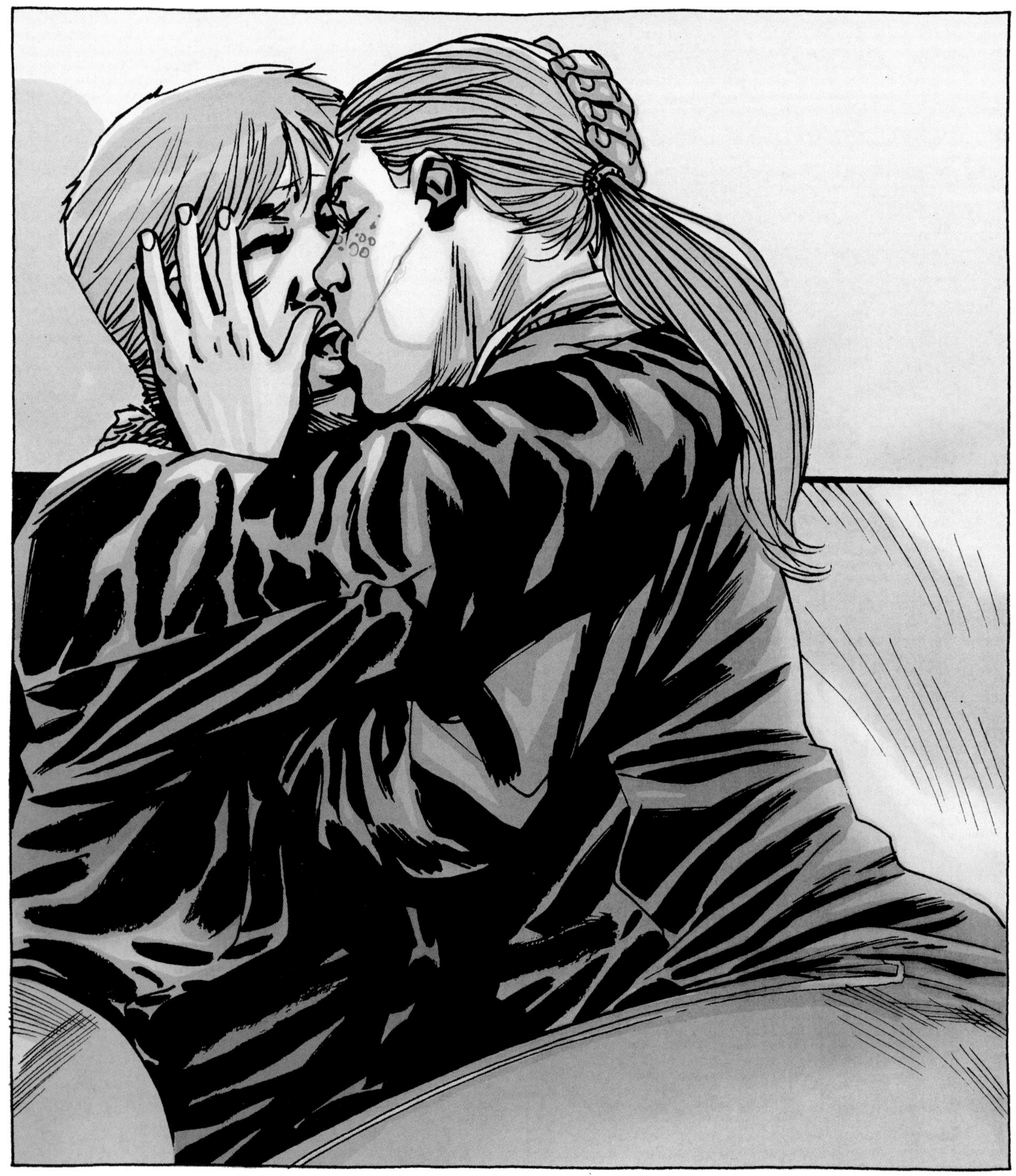

Chapter Sixteen:
A Larger World

ERIC, LOOK OUT!

AGH!
SHIT!
GRAAGH!

THOK!

HUFF!
HUFF!
YOU OKAY?
KEEP YOUR EYES OPEN, PEOPLE! WE'RE OFFICIALLY NOT ALONE OUT HERE.

BLAM!
GAH!

SORRY, AARON-- HE WAS JUST SO CLOSE.
I HAD A CLEAR SHOT, AND...

NO, HEY-- THANKS, MAN.
THAT WAS CLOSE.

A FEW WEEKS INSIDE THE WALLS AND WE CAN'T EVEN WATCH OUR OWN BACKS.
HOW PATHETIC ARE WE?

IS EVERYONE OKAY?!

WE'RE FINE.
EVERYONE'S FINE.

WELL, I'D STILL SAY WE'VE WORN OUT OUR WELCOME HERE.

I THINK WE'VE GOT A PRETTY NICE HAUL. GOOD ENOUGH TO EARN US A TRIP BACK, RIGHT?
AND YOU WERE RIGHT, GLENN. COMING OUT HERE... BEING WITH YOU, SEEING HOW IT'S DONE. IT'S HELPED. I FEEL BETTER ABOUT THINGS.
SAFER... WHICH IS ODD, I KNOW... BUT THIS TRIP HAS REALLY PUT EVERYTHING INTO PERSPECTIVE.

IF EVERYONE'S BACKPACKS ARE AT LEAST HALF AS FULL AS MINE-- WE'RE IN REALLY GOOD SHAPE.
IF WE START DRIVING NOW-- WE SHOULD BE ABLE TO GET BACK BEFORE DARK.

GREAT. I DON'T THINK I COULD TAKE ANOTHER NIGHT SLEEPING IN THE VAN.
CRYBABY.

ALL ABOARD.
AND FAST-- LOOKS LIKE WE'VE GOT MORE COMPANY.

WE'RE GOING TO RUN OUT OF FOOD AGAIN.
NO MATTER HOW MUCH FOOD THEY RETURN WITH... IT'S JUST A MATTER OF TIME.

IT'S BEEN ALMOST TWO YEARS SINCE PEOPLE STOPPED MAKING CANNED GOODS... WE'RE ALREADY PUSHING PAST THE EXPIRATION DATE ON MOST THINGS.
THINGS THAT ARE STILL FRESH, WELL... THEY'RE NOT THE MOST DESIRABLE ITEMS. CANNED FISH SHOULDN'T LAST *THREE YEARS...* Y'KNOW?

I FEEL LIKE WE'LL BE HUNTING WILD DOGS BEFORE THE END OF THE WINTER. WE SIMPLY WERE NOT PREPARED.
THAT'S A MISTAKE I REFUSE TO MAKE A SECOND TIME... WE CAN'T ***AFFORD*** IT.
WE NEED TO GET SERIOUS ABOUT FARMING.

WE NEED TO ASK AROUND, SEE IF THERE'S ANYONE HERE WHO HAS ANY EXPERIENCE WITH IT.
WE'RE GOING TO NEED TO GET SUPPLIES... SEEDS, FERTILIZER, WHATEVER IT IS YOU NEED FOR THIS KIND OF THING.

AS FAR AS LAND GOES, WE COULD JUST PICK THREE OR FOUR YARDS... MORE DEPENDING ON HOW BIG AN AREA WE'D NEED.

THERE ARE STILL ENOUGH VACANT HOUSES WE WOULDN'T NEED TO TAKE OVER ANYONE'S BACKYARDS.
THAT FALLS UNDER... ZONING. SOUNDS LIKE AN ABRAHAM PROBLEM.

I CAN HANDLE THAT, EASY.

I'LL ASK AROUND, SEE IF THERE ARE ANY FARMERS IN THE MIX HERE.
GOOD, I THINK THAT'S ALL FOR TODAY. THANKS FOR COMING, EVERYONE.

WHEN DO YOU THINK MY MOM AND DAD WILL COME BACK?
SUPPOSED TO BE TOMORROW AT THE LATEST, RIGHT? THEY SET A DATE.

DOES THAT HURT?
YOUR EYE?

NO... NEVER DID REALLY.
WEIRD, HUH?

I FEEL BAD FOR YOU... IT'S SO UNFAIR.
NOTHING BAD *EVER* HAPPENS TO ME.

ARE YOU SERIOUS? YOUR DAD *AND* YOUR MOM ARE BOTH DEAD.
GLENN AND MAGGIE ARE JUST TWO PEOPLE WHO TOOK YOU IN.

I'M SORRY. I DIDN'T MEAN TO--
IT'S OKAY, I KNOW...
...I JUST LIKE TO *PRETEND* THINGS ARE DIFFERENT. IT MAKES ME HAPPY.

I'M NOT SAYING ALIENATING HIM IS A GOOD IDEA, BUT YOU'VE REALLY PULLED NICHOLAS INTO THE INNER CIRCLE THESE LAST COUPLE WEEKS.
YOU THINK THAT'S WISE?
KEEP YOUR ENEMIES CLOSER, RIGHT? AND, I'M STILL NOT EVEN CONVINCED HE'S AN ENEMY.

EVER THE OPTIMIST.
SOPHIA AND CARL GETTING ALONG WHILE SHE STAYS HERE?

SURE, THEY'VE ALWAYS BEEN FRIENDS.
SHE'S A LITTLE *WEIRD* AT TIMES, BUT NOTHING WE CAN'T HANDLE.

OKAY, WELL...

I GUESS I'LL BE GOING HOME NOW...
...ALONE.

I SEE YOU STOPPED WEARING DALE'S HAT.

DON'T...
DON'T TRY TO DRIVE ME AWAY. IT'S... TOO UNLIKE YOU.

YOU HAVE TO KNOW... THIS...
...COULD NEVER WORK.

BULLSHIT.

YOU AND I--MORE THAN ANY OTHER COUPLE HERE, HAVE A CHANCE OF MAKING IT WORK.
AFTER ALL WE'VE LIVED THROUGH TOGETHER... ALL WE'VE ***LOST...***
I CAN'T THINK OF TWO PEOPLE AS UNIQUELY COMPATIBLE AS THE TWO OF US. WE ***KNOW*** THIS WORLD--WE KNOW HOW TO ***SURVIVE*** AND--

NO.

JUST... **NO.** OKAY?

I CARE ABOUT YOU... AND ALMOST EVERYONE I'VE CARED ABOUT UP UNTIL NOW... HAS DIED.
I DON'T WANT YOU TO DIE.

HOW'D THE MEETING GO?

GOOD, RICK'S GETTING REALLY GOOD AT BOSSING EVERYONE AROUND.

NO COMMENT.
OH, STOP IT.

STILL, EACH DAY THAT PASSES WITH THAT GROUP OUTSIDE-- IT MAKES ME UNEASY. I WORRY THEY'RE NOT ALL GOING TO COME BACK, OR *NONE* OF THEM WILL.
RICK'S IDEA TO SEND OUT LARGER GROUPS ON LONGER TRIPS MAKES SENSE... BUT...
...I JUST HOPE HE'S RIGHT.

COME ON-- YOU CAN'T STAND HERE ALL DAY.
THERE'S WORK TO BE DONE...

I KNOW...

...IT HAPPENED A LONG TIME AGO. HOW COULD I NOT BE ATTRACTED TO THAT GUY?
HE WAS ALWAYS IN CONTROL, ALWAYS KNEW THE RIGHT THING TO DO--HE WAS ALWAYS... SAVING US.

I'VE FELT THIS WAY FOR A WHILE.

EVEN BEFORE YOU...

NO...

I'M NOT TALKING TO A FUCKING HAT.

I'M SORRY TO BOTHER YOU.
NO BOTHER. I'M JUST DOING AN INVENTORY ON OUR MEDICATION.
I'LL UPDATE THE LIST OF WHAT WE NEED AFTER HEATH AND THE REST RETURN. WHAT CAN I DO FOR YOU?

I KNOW IT'S IMPORTANT TO CLEAN CARL'S WOUND EVERY DAY, BUT HE WON'T LET ME, AND TO BE QUITE HONEST, I FIND IT... DIFFICULT.
IT'S NOT... EASY TO LOOK AT.

CAN YOU BRING HIM BY IN THE NEXT HOUR OR SO? SOUNDS LIKE I NEED TO DO IT TONIGHT.
IT'S REALLY NO PROBLEM FOR ME TO DO IT EVERY DAY. IT'S NOT SOMETHING WE CAN IGNORE IN THIS EARLY STAGE OF HIS HEALING.

THANKS SO MUCH, I--

WHAT IS IT--?
SOMEONE JUST RAN PAST YOUR WINDOW.
EXCUSE ME.

OH... THEY'RE BACK.
IT'S GOOD NEWS. THAT'S REFRESHING.

SO... HOW'D YOU DO?

GOOD, NOT GREAT. WE'LL BE FINE FOR A FEW MORE WEEKS, BUT JUST BARELY.
IT'S SLIM PICKINGS OUT THERE, RICK. I DON'T KNOW HOW WE'RE GOING TO--

WHERE'S SOPHIA?

I LEFT THEM BACK AT THE--

MOM!

SOPHIA! I'M SO HAPPY TO SEE YOU.
DID YOU HAVE FUN STAYING WITH RICK AND CARL?

I DID. BUT PLEASE DON'T GO AWAY AGAIN.
I MISSED YOU.

I UNDERSTAND, DEAR. I'M GLAD YOU HAD FUN. I HAD FUN SEEING WHAT YOUR DADDY DOES WHEN HE GOES OUT.
I'LL BE LESS SCARED WHEN HE GOES OUT NEXT--AND I'LL STAY WITH YOU.

YOU KNOW I'M JUST PRETENDING YOU'RE MY MOM AND DAD, RIGHT?
I'M NOT AS SCARED ANYMORE... SO I CAN TALK ABOUT THAT NOW.

THAT'S VERY BRAVE OF YOU, DEAR.

AND YOU KNOW, IT DOESN'T MEAN WE LOVE YOU ANY LESS THAN A REAL MOMMY AND DADDY.

MAN, I THOUGHT WE'D NEVER GET THAT VAN UNLOADED. WE ENDED UP FINDING QUITE A BIT OF STUFF.
YEAH, AND WHY EXACTLY DID WE HELP UNLOAD EVERYTHING? I SAW GLENN AND MAGGIE SCURRYING AWAY AS SOON AS WE GOT THERE.

ERIC, BE NICE. THEY SPENT A WEEK AWAY FROM THEIR DAUGHTER, I CAN UNDERSTAND.

FINE, FINE. BESIDES, IT MAKES ME FEEL A LITTLE LESS GUILTY ABOUT KEEPING THIS A SECRET.

ERIC! WHY WOULD YOU--YOU KNOW WE'RE SUPPOSED TO SHARE THINGS LIKE THAT.

THE GROUP WOULD HAVE WANTED TO DRINK THE WHOLE BOTTLE BEFORE WE GOT BACK ANYWAY-- AND BESIDES, THIS SCOTCH IS TWENTY YEARS OLD.
I DON'T THINK ANYONE BUT US WOULD BE ABLE TO *APPRECIATE* IT.

I FEEL SO ASHAMED OF YOU, BUT I'M SURE THAT WILL WEAR OFF IN THE TIME IT TAKES ME TO GET A COUPLE GLASSES.
SO FORGIVING, THAT'S WHY I LOVE YOU.

CARL, WHAT ARE YOU DOING?
READING.

YOU KNOW WE'RE NOT SUPPOSED TO BE USING LIGHTS AT NIGHT. WE NEED TO CONSERVE POWER.
THE PANELS DON'T ABSORB ENOUGH SOLAR POWER IN THE WINTER TO BEGIN WITH--AND WE'RE RUNNING A LOT OF HEATERS.

IT'S JUST A LAMP, DAD. AND...
...
I'M TURNING IT OFF.

SORRY.
CLICK.

HOW'S YOUR EYE--DID IT HURT WHEN DOCTOR CLOYD CLEANED IT?

A LITTLE.
DON'T CALL IT AN EYE--I DON'T HAVE AN EYE THERE ANYMORE.

I'M SORRY, I DON'T... KNOW WHAT TO CALL IT, THEN.

IT'S A HOLE. I HAVE A BIG GIANT HOLE IN MY HEAD WHERE AN EYE USED TO BE.
I'M GOING TO CALL IT A HOLE.

LOOK, I KNOW THIS ISN'T EASY AND I KNOW YOU'RE DEALING WITH A LOT RIGHT NOW, BUT, SON...
THERE'S NO REASON TO GET SHORT WITH ME.

YOU DON'T KNOW ANYTHING.

EXCUSE ME?

YOU DON'T KNOW HOW THIS FEELS. YOU DON'T KNOW WHAT IT'S LIKE TO SEE YOUR FACE IN THE MIRROR AND THINK IT'S GROSS.
YOU DON'T KNOW HOW HARD IT IS TO READ WITH ONE EYE... YOU DON'T KNOW ANYTHING ABOUT MY PROBLEM.
YOU DON'T KNOW ANYTHING ABOUT WHAT'S HAPPENED TO ME.

YOU'RE RIGHT, SON.
YOU'RE RIGHT.
I'M SORRY.

AAGH!

CARL?!
WHAT HAPPENED?

I... HAD A BAD DREAM.

IT'S OKAY, YOU JUST STARTLED ME THERE.

IT WAS HORRIBLE, DAD.
THERE WAS THIS BOY... AND HE WAS YOUNGER THAN ME...

...AND I SHOT HIM.
HE WAS BAD, I KNEW IT JUST FROM LOOKING AT HIM... BUT I *KILLED* HIM.

IT DIDN'T *FEEL* LIKE A DREAM.
I SAW HIS BRAIN PARTS, IT WASN'T LIKE IN A VIDEO GAME...

I'M SORRY I WAS MEAN TO YOU TONIGHT.
I GET FRUSTRATED SOMETIMES, AND...
I'M JUST SORRY...

IT'S OKAY.
WE CAN TALK IN THE MORNING IF YOU'D LIKE. JUST GO BACK TO SLEEP.

IS THERE ANY COFFEE?
GUYS DIDN'T COME BACK WITH MUCH OF THE THINGS THAT THEY DID FIND... BUT THEY COULDN'T FIND ANY COFFEE.
WHICH SUCKS.

TELL ME ABOUT IT.
CARL WOKE UP FROM A NIGHTMARE LAST NIGHT AND... I JUST COULDN'T GET BACK TO SLEEP.

WAKING UP FROM A NIGHTMARE? MAN... WOULDN'T THAT BE A NICE THING FOR ALL OF US TO DO?

ARMORY OPEN? NEED THE HEAVY STUFF FOR TODAY.
WEDNESDAY, RIGHT? I UNLOCKED IT FOR YOU.

YOU GUYS BE CAREFUL OUT THERE, OKAY?
HOW MANY YOU TAKING OUT?

JUST MICHONNE AND I. IT'S BEEN PRETTY LIGHT THESE LAST COUPLE WEEKS. BETTER IF WE'RE NOT TRIPPING OVER EACH OTHER DOING IT.
I THINK IT'LL BE FASTER JUST THE TWO OF US. WE'LL SEE HOW IT GOES.

BROUGHT YOU SOMETHING.

THANKS, THINK I'LL NEED **TWO** GUNS?
GOING OUT ON OUR OWN FOR THE FIRST TIME... I'M NOT TAKING ANY CHANCES.

I FIGURE ON OUR FIRST PERIMETER CHECK, IF IT'S PRETTY CROWDED, WE POP BACK IN FOR ANDREA, MAYBE HOLLY... NICHOLAS.

OF COURSE. HAVE A GOOD NIGHT LAST NIGHT?

NOT REALLY.
I'M PRETTY LONELY.

HOLY SHIT... I WAS JUST MAKING CONVERSATION. I DIDN'T EXPECT YOU TO BE DEPRESSINGLY HONEST.
NO POINT IN LYING. WHY'D YOU ASK IF YOU DON'T *CARE?*

WHOA, I NEVER SAID I DIDN'T CARE.
JUST CAUGHT ME A LITTLE OFF GUARD. FUCK.

LOOKS LIKE NOTHING'S GOTTEN THROUGH.

DON'T TRY TO CHANGE THE FUCKING SUBJECT ON ME. YOU'RE LONELY.
WANNA TALK ABOUT IT?

TALK? SURE. I'D LOVE TO TALK ABOUT IT.
ANY EXCUSE TO TALK, REALLY. I FIND THAT I JUST DON'T HAVE A LOT TO SAY ANYMORE. I USED TO TALK FOR A LIVING, MORE OR LESS.
I SPENT SO MUCH TIME ALONE BEFORE I MET UP WITH RICK AND THE OTHERS... I JUST GOT USED TO NOT TALKING.

NOT THAT I DIDN'T TALK AT ALL WHEN I WAS... *ALONE.*
BUT I'M NOT GETTING INTO THAT...

YOU KNOW, IF YOU'RE JUST LONELY, YOU COULD GET TOGETHER WITH HOLLY AND I ANY TIME.
OPEN INVITATION.

NO WAY.
I HAVEN'T DONE ANYTHING LIKE THAT SINCE COLLEGE.

WHOA, I MEANT FOR DINNER... BUT... UH...
SLOW DOWN. I WAS JOKING.
AND GROSS.

NO ONE HERE ACTUALLY KNOWS ME.
AND WHOSE GODDAMN FAULT IS THAT?

LET'S CHECK THE ALLEYS FIRST.

FIRST ONE.
YOU OR ME?

GRUH.
YOU.
SHOULD KEEP THINGS QUIET UNTIL WE'RE SURE THERE'S NOT A SWARM OF THEM NEARBY.

SUITS ME.

SHUKK!

COVER ME.
I'LL MAKE THIS QUICK.

SHUKK!

WHUD!

SVASH!

BRAKKA! BRAKKA!

YOU WERE TAKING TOO FUCKING LONG.

WHOA, THANKS.
I THOUGHT I'D NEVER GET A CLEAR SHOT AT GETTING OUT OF HERE. SLEEPING IN AN ABANDONED CAR IS NO PICNIC, BUT WAKING UP TO BE SURROUNDED BY EMPTIES... HEH, THAT'S--

WHO ARE YOU AND WHAT ARE YOU DOING HERE?!
RELAX, I JUST WANT TO TALK.

WITHOUT A SWORD IN MY FACE.
KRAK!

ACK!

WHAT THE FUCK?!

SERIOUSLY, DUDE. PLEASE DON'T SHOOT ME.
I HAVE NO IDEA WHAT MIGHT HAPPEN TO MY HAND IF I WERE TO SUDDENLY DIE. THAT CAUSES SPASMS, RIGHT?

HONESTLY, I REALLY JUST WANT TO TALK. THE TWO OF YOU SEEM PRETTY HOT-HEADED.
IS THERE SOMEONE SLIGHTLY MORE CALM, WHO I COULD POSSIBLY HAVE A DISCUSSION WITH?

ACK!
WRAMM!

ASSHOLE.
KRAK!

DON'T PLAY WITH HIM--JUST GET OUT OF THE WAY!

SHIT!

BRAKKA! BRAKKA! BRAKKA!

FUCK!
BRAKKA! BRAKKA!

BRAKKA! BRAKKA! BRAKKA!

YOU SEE HIM?

STAY BEHIND ME, I'LL COVER YOU.
HE'S JUST GOT THE SWORD, RIGHT?
THINK SO.

YOU'RE QUICK-- I'LL GIVE YOU THAT. BUT THERE'S NO DAMN WAY YOU'RE BULLETPROOF.
IF YOU AIN'T CAUGHT ONE YET, YOU KNOW IT'S ONLY A MATTER OF TIME.

SO WHY DON'T YOU...?

LOOK OUT!

WRAKK!

BLAM!
KRAK!

WHACK!

DAMN IT.

...

REALLY, I'VE JUST ABOUT HAD ENOUGH OF THIS. ONE OF US IS GOING TO GET KILLED... AND AS MUCH AS I'D PREFER IT NOT BE ME... I DON'T WANT IT TO BE ONE OF YOU GUYS EITHER.
SO, GOD DAMN IT-- BEFORE THIS GETS UGLY...
TAKE ME TO YOUR LEADER.

JUST...
...GO GET RICK.

LOCK THE GATE! WHO KNOWS HOW MANY OF THEM THERE ARE!
GET EVERYONE ARMED AND READY! WE GOTTA PREPARE FOR ANYTHING.

WHERE ARE THEY?
DOWN THE ALLEY, RIGHT HERE!

THIS IS YOUR LEADER? LOOKS LIKE HE'D WEIGH A BUCK THIRTY, SOAKING WET.
YOU MUST BE ONE HELL OF A BAD ASS TO BE BOSSING AROUND MISTER BEEFCAKE HERE.
LET HIM GO.

DON'T MAKE ME ASK AGAIN.

CAN DO, I JUST ASK THAT YOU LOWER THAT GUN.
IT'S JUST NOT SAFE TO KEEP THOSE THINGS POINTED AT PEOPLE. I'M NOT ASKING YOU TO GET RID OF IT, I DON'T WANT YOU TO FEEL THREATENED, I ONLY WANT TO TALK.

OKAY THEN...
CLINK.

HEY!

WRAMM!

TALK. A CONVERSATION... THAT'S ALL I'M HERE FOR.

STAND WHERE YOU ARE.
I CAN SEE I DON'T WANT YOU ANYWHERE NEAR ME-- ARMED OR NOT.

UNDERSTOOD, I THINK THAT'S ENOUGH FIGHTING. PLEASE ALLOW ME TO INTRODUCE MYSELF.
MY NAME IS PAUL MONROE...
...BUT MY FRIENDS HAVE TAKEN TO CALLING ME *JESUS.*

HOW MANY "FRIENDS" DO YOU HAVE IN YOUR GROUP?
I WOULDN'T CONSIDER THEM ALL FRIENDS-- BUT I COME FROM A LARGE COMMUNITY... ALMOST TWO HUNDRED.

WHERE ARE THEY?
WHAT DO YOU WANT?
WE WANT EVERYTHING YOU HAVE... WHATEVER IT IS YOU HAVE TO OFFER, I'M SURE WE COULD USE IT.
MAN, THAT DOESN'T SOUND RIGHT. I'M USUALLY BETTER AT THIS. WE DON'T WANT TO TAKE ANYTHING FROM YOU...

LET ME JUST START OVER, GUYS.
I DIDN'T MEAN TO PICK A FIGHT WITH YOU. I STARTED TALKING-- AND SUDDENLY I HAD A SWORD IN MY FACE. I HAVE A THING ABOUT WEAPONS BEING POINTED AT ME... I REALLY CAN'T STAND IT.
I'M SURE YOU CAN UNDERSTAND.
I SHOULDN'T HAVE ATTACKED YOU, I REACTED BEFORE I'D REALLY THOUGHT ABOUT IT.
THEN THINGS JUST SPIRALED OUT OF CONTROL. MY FAULT, I KNOW... BUT I TRIED REASONING WITH YOU. I TRIED TO STOP IT.

THAT EVEN REMOTELY CLOSE TO WHAT HAPPENED?
HE CAME OUT OF A PARKED CAR AFTER I'D TAKEN OUT A FEW ROAMERS. HE STARTLED ME... AND YEAH, THAT'S PRETTY MUCH IT.

MY GROUP LIVES IN AN AREA ABOUT TWENTY MILES FROM HERE, JUST ON THE OTHER SIDE OF WASHINGTON.
IT'S A GOOD COMMUNITY, LOTS OF NICE PEOPLE THERE. IT'S A GREAT PLACE TO LIVE... BUT LIKE I SAY, THERE'S ALMOST TWO HUNDRED PEOPLE THERE.
WE'RE ALWAYS IN NEED OF SUPPLIES.

WE DON'T HAVE A LOT TO GIVE, BUT I PROMISE YOU WE'LL PUT UP A STRONG FIGHT TO KEEP YOU FROM IT.

AGAIN... WE'RE NOT LOOKING TO TAKE ANYTHING. I'D LIKE TO ESTABLISH A TRADE RELATIONSHIP BETWEEN YOUR GROUP AND MINE.
I'M SURE WE HAVE THINGS YOU COULD USE--AND YOU HAVE THINGS WE COULD USE.

LIKE WHAT?

WELL, FOR INSTANCE-- I DON'T KNOW HOW YOU HAVEN'T RUN OUT OF AMMO YET, BUT IF YOU'VE GOT SOME KIND OF HOOK-UP, OUR GUNS RAN DRY A LONG TIME AGO. I CARRY THEM AROUND FOR SHOW.
SO WHATEVER YOU COULD SPARE WOULD BE VERY VALUABLE TO US.
AND WHAT DO YOU HAVE?

WELL, WE'VE BUILT AROUND A FARM, SO WE'RE PRETTY STOCKED UP ON VARIOUS FOOD PRODUCTS.
BUT IF YOU'RE WELL STOCKED, WE HAVE CLOTHING, TOOLS AND PLENTY OF OTHER ITEMS IN THE OFFING.

YOU EXPECT ME TO BELIEVE ALL YOUR PEOPLE ARE INTERESTED IN... IS FINDING NEW *PARTNERS* TO TRADE WITH?

WELL, IT'S THE TRUTH-- SO YES.

AND YOU CAME ALL THE WAY HERE... JUST TO LET US KNOW ABOUT THIS?

NOT EXACTLY. I SCOUT FOR NEW GROUPS, *YES*-- BUT I HAD TO MAKE A FEW SUPPLY DROPS AT A COUPLE OTHER COMMUNITIES ON MY WAY HERE.
THERE'S A PLACE A FEW MILES WEST, THEY SAID THEY'D HEARD GUNFIRE WHILE SCOUTING NEAR HERE--BUT COULDN'T FIND YOU.

DID YOU SAY TWO *OTHER* COMMUNITIES? THERE'S YOU AND TWO OTHERS?

WAIT A MINUTE...
DO YOU GUYS THINK YOU'RE THE ONLY SURVIVORS OUT HERE?
BOY... YOUR WORLD IS CERTAINLY ABOUT TO *CHANGE.*

WE DON'T THINK WE'RE THE ONLY SURVIVORS LEFT... BUT WE HAVEN'T EXACTLY RUN INTO MANY ORGANIZED GROUPS.
LET ME GET THIS STRAIGHT-- YOU'VE GOT A NETWORK OF COMMUNITIES THAT TRADE GOODS AND COMMUNICATE WITH EACH OTHER?
AND YOU'D LIKE US TO JOIN THIS COMMUNITY?

THAT'S EXACTLY RIGHT.

OKAY. WHAT'S THE NEXT STEP FOR US THEN?

I'LL ESCORT SOME OF YOUR GROUP BACK TO THE HILLTOP SO YOU CAN SEE WHAT WE HAVE TO OFFER AND INTRODUCE YOU TO GREGORY, HE'S THE GUY IN CHARGE.
I'LL SHOW YOU A CLEAR ROUTE BETWEEN HERE AND THE HILLTOP YOU CAN USE FOR TRADE-- GET YOU SET UP.

OKAY THEN. SOUNDS SIMPLE ENOUGH. LET'S GET STARTED.

REALLY? THAT WAS *EASY.*

HOW COULD WE REFUSE?

WHA--?!

WRAMM!

WHY DID--?

KRAK!

TIE HIM UP BEFORE HE COMES TO.

I DON'T WANT TO PUT THE WHOLE COMMUNITY IN A PANIC, SO WE'RE GOING TO KEEP THIS BETWEEN US FOR NOW.
WE'VE GOT A MAN HELD IN THE BACK OF THE INFIRMARY. HE CLAIMS HE'S FROM A MUCH LARGER COMMUNITY THAT WANTS TO NEGOTIATE SOME KIND OF TRADE DEAL WITH US.
I DON'T BUY IT.
HE'S SAYING THERE'S ROUGHLY TWO-HUNDRED PEOPLE IN HIS GROUP. IF THAT'S TRUE, THEY COULD BE PREPARING FOR AN ATTACK AT ANY MOMENT.
I DON'T WANT TO NEEDLESSLY ALARM ANYONE. RIGHT NOW, WE'RE JUST PREPARING FOR THE WORST.
IF THEY WANT THIS PLACE-- WE'RE NOT GOING DOWN WITHOUT A FIGHT.

I NEED EVERYONE TO MOVE QUICKLY. IF THIS IS GOING TO HAPPEN, IT COULD HAPPEN **SOON.**
HERE'S WHAT I NEED YOU ALL TO DO.

ABRAHAM, YOU'RE ON PERIMETER WATCH. I WANT YOU TO START PLACING PEOPLE ON THE WALL, ARMED, KEEPING WATCH.
TELL THEM TO STAY LOW, OUT OF SIGHT.

ANDREA, I NEED YOU UP IN THE TOWER. YOU'VE GOT A CLEAR VANTAGE POINT OF THE SURROUNDING AREA UP THERE. IF YOU SEE SOMETHING WHEN YOU GET IN PLACE, FIRE OFF A WARNING SHOT.
IF YOU SEE NOTHING, JUST SIT TIGHT AND WATCH THE AREA.

MICHONNE, FIRST, YOU'RE GOING TO ESCORT ANDREA TO THE TOWER, I DON'T WANT ANYONE OUT THERE ALONE.
ONCE SHE'S IN PLACE AND YOU'RE SURE YOU WEREN'T SEEN, COME BACK HERE AND HELP ABRAHAM WITH PERIMETER WATCH.

OLIVIA, I WANT YOU TO DO AN UPDATED INVENTORY ON GUNS AND AMMO. WHAT WE HAVE, WHERE IT IS, HOW LOW WE ARE ON THINGS.
CHECK IN WITH EVERYONE, SEE WHAT THEY'RE KEEPING IN THEIR HOMES. DON'T LET ON WHY YOU'RE DOING IT, JUST GET THE INFORMATION.

EUGENE, YOU'RE A SMART GUY. WE'RE RUNNING OUT OF AMMO, IT'S INEVITABLE. YOUR JOB IS TO COME UP WITH ALTERNATIVES.
IN THE SHORT TERM, WHAT DO WE HAVE TO HELP US DEFEND THIS PLACE... KEEP PEOPLE OFF THE WALLS? BOILING OIL KIND OF STUFF.

DENISE, JUST GET THE INFIRMARY READY, PREPARE A TRIAGE CENTER OF SOME KIND. AN ARMY OF ROAMERS IS ONE THING... AN ARMY OF PEOPLE IS ANOTHER.
BE READY FOR ANYTHING.

I DID AN INVENTORY NOT TOO LONG AGO ON OUR AMMUNITION. WE WERE RUNNING LOW THEN. WE FOUND SOME WHEN THE GROUP WAS OUT LAST WEEK, BUT...
WE JUST DON'T HAVE ENOUGH TO HOLD OFF ANY KIND OF ASSAULT.
I *KNOW*.
YOU LET ME WORRY ABOUT THAT. YOU JUST FIND OUT *EXACTLY* HOW DIRE THINGS ARE.

I'M ON TOP OF IT.
RICK, JUST A MOMENT, PLEASE.
YEAH? YOU ALREADY GOT SOMETHING FOR ME?

NOT YET, NO. I HAVE IDEAS... BUT NOTHING CONCRETE. THERE ARE--JUST TAKE COMFORT KNOWING THERE ARE A LOT OF OPTIONS. I'M JUST ORGANIZING MY THOUGHTS NOW, I'LL PRESENT YOU WITH A DETAILED LIST SHORTLY.
NEED TO GET ALL MY DUCKS IN A ROW.
ASSUMING WE GET THROUGH THIS... I COULD GET US UP AND RUNNING VERY SHORTLY.
LONG TERM, THOUGH... I JUST WANTED TO LET YOU KNOW, IT'S NOT IMPOSSIBLE FOR US TO MAKE OUR OWN BULLETS. WE'D NEED TO START SAVING OUR SPENT CASINGS, I KNOW A LITTLE BIT ABOUT BULLET RELOADING AND CASTING IS NOT THE MOST COMPLEX PROCESS.

BEST NEWS I'VE HEARD ALL DAY. THAT WOULD CERTAINLY FIX A FEW OF OUR PROBLEMS.
I'M LOOKING FORWARD TO HEARING MORE WHEN YOU'RE READY.

THANKS.
IT'LL FEEL GOOD... TO BE PULLING MY WEIGHT AROUND HERE.
YEAH.

RICK?

I'M HEADING OUT NOW.
BEFORE I GO, I JUST WANTED TO SAY, I KNOW YOU'RE JUST BEING CAUTIOUS... AND THAT'S GOOD. YOU **SHOULD** BE.
BUT THIS GUY'S OFFERING US SUPPLIES, AND FROM WHAT YOU SAY, HE COULD JUST BE TRYING TO MAKE CONTACT WITH US. AND THAT CAN'T BE EASY, SO...

WHAT ARE YOU SAYING?

WHAT IF HE'S **RIGHT?**
IF HE'S PART OF THIS COMMUNITY... AND WHAT HE'S SAYING IS TRUE, THE LAST THING WE'D WANT TO DO IS PISS THEM OFF.

HOW LONG DO YOU PLAN ON KEEPING ME HERE LIKE THIS?

AS LONG AS WE HAVE TO.

I GET IT, Y'KNOW. IT'S SCARY OUT HERE IN THE WORLD. YOU GOT A GUY TELLING YOU ABOUT A BETTER PLACE, A NEW WAY OF LIFE...
WHY WOULD YOU BELIEVE HIM?
I DO THIS BECAUSE I CAN HANDLE IT, THIS JOB. I TRY NOT TO TAKE IT PERSONALLY... YOU'RE JUST TRYING TO PROTECT YOUR PEOPLE. JUST DO YOUR DIGGING AND DON'T KEEP ME TIED UP FOR LONG.
I'D RATHER NOT END UP PISSING MYSELF.

HOW CLOSE IS YOUR GROUP?
WHEN DO THEY PLAN TO ATTACK?

MAN... MY GROUP IS TWENTY MILES AWAY...
...AND THEY DON'T ATTACK ANYONE.

I'M SORRY...
...BUT I JUST DON'T BELIEVE YOU.

WELL?
SEE ANYTHING?

NO. NOTHING.
ALL'S QUIET. A FEW ROAMERS HERE AND THERE... NOTHING TO WORRY ABOUT.
NO LARGE GROUPS, NO SIGN OF ANY GATHERING ARMIES AS FAR AS THE EYE CAN SEE.

RICK... DID YOU TALK TO HIM?

I DID. HE SPEAKS CLEARLY AND CONFIDENTLY, EVEN THOUGH HE'S RESTRAINED, HELPLESS. THAT'S NOT A GOOD SIGN TO ME.
THE GUILTY MAN SLEEPS IN HIS CELL WHILE THE INNOCENT ONE CLIMBS UP THE WALLS WITH WORRY... UNABLE TO RELAX.
HE'S HIDING SOMETHING.
HIS DEMEANOR IS SETTING OFF ALL KINDS OF ALARMS.

AND YET... I DON'T SEE ANYTHING OUT HERE THAT SHOULD CAUSE US ANY CONCERN.

MAYBE THEY KNOW YOUR LINE OF SIGHT AND ARE AVOIDING IT.
MAYBE WE'RE NOT LOOKING HARD ENOUGH.

EUGENE? WHAT'S GOING ON? WE'RE ALL OUT OF OUR MINDS WITH WORRY ABOUT THIS NEW GROUP AND YOU'RE *EXCITED* ABOUT SOMETHING?
RICK'S GOT EVERYTHING UNDER CONTROL. WHEN ARE YOU GOING TO REALIZE THAT?
I'VE GOT A PLAN THAT WILL HELP US--A WAY TO REPLENISH OUR AMMUNITION. I FOUND A PLACE IN THE PHONE BOOK THAT'S NEARBY, SHOULD HAVE THE MAJORITY OF WHAT I NEED.
I'M GOING TO GET ABRAHAM TO TAKE ME OVER THERE.

HOLLY COMING, TOO?

ROSITA, PLEASE. JUST *FORGET* HIM, OKAY?
HE NEVER CARED FOR YOU... NOT LIKE YOU DID FOR HIM...

...NOT LIKE I DO.

I KNOW YOU'VE BEEN LONELY THESE LAST FEW WEEKS. I COULD MAKE YOU HAPPY... I KNOW WHAT YOU LIKE.
IF YOU WOULD ONLY LET ME *TRY*.
EUGENE...
I'M SORRY.

MAKE NO MISTAKE... WE'RE *BAIT.*
ANDREA DOESN'T THINK THESE PEOPLE ARE OUT THERE... SHE CAN'T SEE THEM. IF THEY'RE THERE, WE'RE GOING TO DRAW THEM OUT.
SHE'S WATCHING OVER US-- WE'LL STAY IN HER LINE OF SIGHT, SHE SHOULD BE ABLE TO COVER OUR RETREAT BACK TO THE COMMUNITY IF THEY ATTACK US.
BUT... STAY ALERT.

SO WE GET SHOT, AND THEN OUR PEOPLE ON THE OTHER SIDE OF THE WALL KNOW THEY'RE FUCKED.
THAT THE IDEA?
YOU MIGHT JUST BE A SHITTY LEADER, RICK.
IF ANDREA'S RIGHT, THERE'S NOT A SOUL OUT HERE.
EVEN IF SHE'S WRONG, IDEA IS WE DON'T GET SHOT... *THEY* DO.

OKAY, WE'RE BAIT... BUT DO WE REALLY WANT THEM TO HEAR US COMING WITH ENOUGH TIME TO AMBUSH US? WE SHOULD PROBABLY CUT THE CHATTER.
NOTED.

SHUKK!

DON'T GO TOO FAR AWAY... I CAN'T SEE YOU.

ANYTHING?
NO.

AREA'S CLEAR.
I'M NOT READY TO GIVE UP. KEEP MOVING.

DAMN IT.

STAY CLOSE, KEEP QUIET.
IF THEY'RE OUT HERE... IN HIDING... THEY SHOULD BE CLOSE.

KEEP YOUR EYES OUT FOR ANY NEW SIGNS OF SCAVENGING. IF THEY WERE OUT HERE--THEY WOULD HAVE LOOKED FOR SUPPLIES.
LOOK FOR ANYTHING DISTURBED, ANYTHING THAT'S BEEN MOVED RECENTLY.
LOOK AROUND US. NO ONE'S BEEN THROUGH HERE IN MONTHS, RICK.

THEN WE DOUBLE BACK, HEAD TOWARDS THE COMMUNITY--BUT THROUGH A DIFFERENT AREA.
THEY'RE OUT HERE.
RICK?

DAMN!

RICK, STEP ASIDE.

NO!
WE GOTTA KEEP THINGS QUIET!
GRAH!

WRAMM!

WHUD!

KRAK!
KRAK!

SVAASH!
WRAKK!

NO.
I CAN DO THIS.

SVAASH!

MICHONNE?
ABRAHAM?

OKAY...
SHUKK!

WROK!

MY GOD... WHAT ARE WE *DOING?*
I DON'T FOLLOW.

THIS.
WE'RE STILL DOING *THIS.*
AFTER ALL THIS TIME... PUTTING OURSELVES IN DANGER... KILLING THE DEAD. THIS IS OUR LIFE? *THIS?*
THINK ABOUT IT... ANYBODY BREAK A SWEAT JUST NOW? I WAS ABOUT AS STARTLED BY THIS AS I WOULD BE CHANGING A TIRE.
THIS PART... THE DEAD WALKING... DEALING WITH THAT... WE'VE GOT THAT DOWN.

NOW I THINK IT'S TIME... FOR SOMETHING ELSE.
THIS GUY, JESUS... HIS PEOPLE ARE EITHER WAITING TO ATTACK US OR THEY'RE NOT. TRUTH BE TOLD... I'M NOT EVEN SCARED OF THAT.
MAYBE THIS IS ARROGANCE, BUT AFTER EVERYTHING... I FEEL LIKE WE'D HAVE A HARD TIME FINDING *ANYONE* MORE DANGEROUS THAN *WE* ARE.
I THINK THAT...

RICK?
C'MON...

THIS WAY.
OUR COMMUNITY IS SAFE. THE WALLS ARE STRONG, WE CAN MAKE A LIFE HERE. BUT WE NEED RESOURCES AND A STEADY STREAM OF SUPPLIES TO KEEP US GOING.

MAYBE THAT'S OUT THERE... OTHER GROUPS. COMMUNITIES LIKE OURS... LIKE HE SAYS.
WE COULD BE SCARED OF IT, LIKE I WAS AT FIRST.

OR WE CAN LOOK AT IT AS AN OPPORTUNITY, A WAY TO KEEP US GOING, WE COULD WORK WITH THESE PEOPLE OUT THERE, MAKE OUR WORLD SAFER, OUR LIVES BETTER.

IT'S SAFE BEHIND THOSE WALLS, BUT I THINK WE'VE LOST SIGHT OF WHAT'S OUT THERE ON THE OTHER SIDE...

...A LARGER WORLD.
LOOK AT IT... IT'S ALL AROUND US, WAITING ON US TO BECOME A PART OF IT AGAIN.
WE JUST HAVE TO BE BRAVE ENOUGH TO ACCEPT IT.

THERE'S A CHANCE THIS GUY IS RIGHT. WE WERE CAUTIOUS, BUT WE HAVEN'T FOUND HIS PEOPLE OUT HERE. THEY AREN'T WAITING TO STRIKE.
ALL INDICATIONS ARE THAT HE'S TELLING THE TRUTH.
IF THEY END UP BEING GOOD PEOPLE, WE'LL WORK WITH THEM...

...IF NOT, WE'LL JUST *TAKE* EVERYTHING THEY HAVE AND LEAVE THEM FOR DEAD.

THERE YOU GO, ALL CLEAN.
EVERYTHING FEELING OKAY?

HURTS A LITTLE SOMETIMES. I CAN HANDLE IT THOUGH.
DOCTOR CLOYD, WHO'S THAT MAN IN THE BACK?

UM...
WELL...

THAT MAN IS A VISITOR, THAT, WELL...
WE'RE KEEPING HIM SAFE, AND, *UH*...

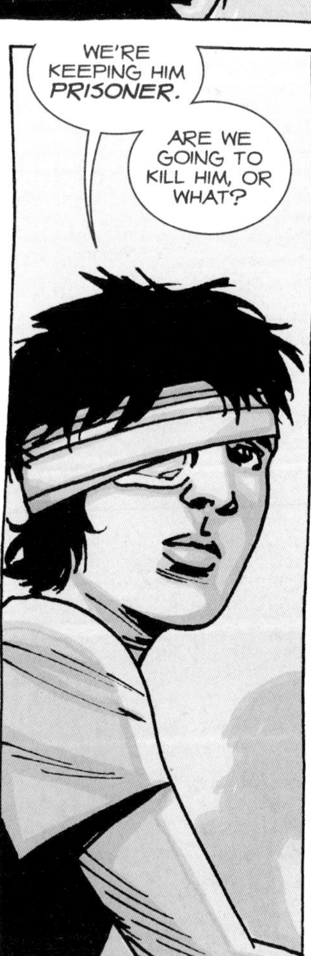
WE'RE KEEPING HIM ***PRISONER.***
ARE WE GOING TO KILL HIM, OR WHAT?

CARL, I DON'T THINK YOUR FATHER--

NEVER MIND. I'LL JUST ASK HIM WHEN HE COMES BACK.

YOU CAN FIND YOUR WAY HOME?
YEP. THANKS. BYE.

UH...
COME ON IN...

I WON'T *BITE.*

WHO ARE YOU!?

FRIENDS CALL ME JESUS. TAKE A SEAT, I'LL TELL YOU WHATEVER YOU WANT TO KNOW.

THEY'RE ALONE.
SO FAR, SO GOOD.

WHAT'S THE WORD?
WE'RE CLEAR. SEEMS LIKE THE GUY IS TELLING THE TRUTH.
RECKON WE'LL BELIEVE HIM FOR NOW. STAND DOWN, LET'S HEAD BACK.

I TAKE IT NOBODY WAS OUT THERE WAITING TO ATTACK...
THIS GUY'S STORY CHECKS OUT, FOR NOW. WE'RE GOING TO GO BACK TO HIS PLACE WITH HIM. PACK SOME THINGS, I WANT YOU WITH ME.
I'D FEEL SAFER OUT THERE WITH YOU BY MY SIDE.

OH, OKAY. WHATEVER YOU NEED, MAN.

GLENN, *WAIT.*

HAVE YOU SEEN CARL?

SAW HIM GO INTO THE INFIRMARY--

CARL!

JESUS SEEMS LIKE A GOOD GUY, DAD. I DON'T THINK WE NEED TO HAVE HIM ALL TIED UP.
I'D LISTEN TO THE BOY...

YOU'RE NOT SUPPOSED TO BE IN HERE.

IF HE WAS A BAD GUY, I WOULD HAVE SHOT HIM.

HE'S JOKING, RIGHT?

HERE'S WHAT'S GOING TO HAPPEN. YOU'RE GOING TO STAY TIED UP, BECAUSE I'VE HEARD WHAT YOU CAN DO ON THE LOOSE.
YOU'RE GOING TO DIRECT US TO YOUR PLACE-- THIS... HILLTOP, WHATEVER YOU CALL IT.
IF I DON'T LIKE WHAT I SEE WHEN WE GET THERE, IF YOU TRY TO ALERT THEM TO OUR ARRIVAL SOMEHOW... I KILL YOU ON THE SPOT.

IF THAT'S THE WAY IT'S GOT TO BE, WHAT OTHER CHOICE DO I HAVE?

NONE.
GOOD THAT YOU KNOW THAT.

HOW LONG YOU KEEPING HIM TIED UP?
AS LONG AS I FEEL WE NEED TO.

WHAT DOES IT MATTER, AARON?

RICK, LOOK--I KNOW YOU'RE JUST TRYING TO KEEP US SAFE, AND FOR WHAT IT'S WORTH, YOU'RE GOOD AT THAT...
...BUT YOU DECKED ME WHEN I INVITED YOUR PEOPLE TO COME HERE. IT'S KIND OF YOUR THING.

I DIDN'T TRUST YOU AT FIRST, EITHER. WHAT'S THE POINT?

MY OFFER TURNED OUT TO BE LEGIT. YOU WERE WRONG TO DOUBT ME. I JUST WORRY--YOU PUSH BACK TOO HARD, AND THIS GUY'S OFFER IS LEGIT, TOO...
...MAYBE YOU DRIVE HIM AWAY.

OR WORSE... MAKE THEM ENEMIES, TURN THEM INTO WHAT YOU'RE SCARED THEY ALREADY ARE.

I HEAR YOU. I DO.
I'M ONLY TAKING THIS AS FAR AS I ABSOLUTELY HAVE TO. JUST... TRUST ME.

I'M HEADING OUT. I DON'T WANT TO WASTE ANY MORE TIME. JESUS IS GOING TO TAKE US TO HIS PEOPLE. WE'RE PACKING UP NOW.
I'M READY WHENEVER YOU ARE.

NO, LOOK. I KIND OF FEEL LIKE I *HAVE* TO GO ON THIS ONE. I CAN'T STAY HERE.
AND YOU'RE REALLY THE PERSON I'D FEEL MOST COMFORTABLE LEAVING CARL WITH. MAGGIE WILL WATCH HIM-- BUT I'D FEEL *MUCH* BETTER KNOWING YOU WERE KEEPING THIS PLACE SAFE.

BULLSHIT. ABRAHAM AND THE REST WILL DO JUST FINE KEEPING THIS PLACE SAFE.
WHOEVER LEAVES WILL BE IN THE REAL DANGER. YOU'RE GOING TO *NEED* ME.

ANDREA, PLEASE...
I'M GOING.

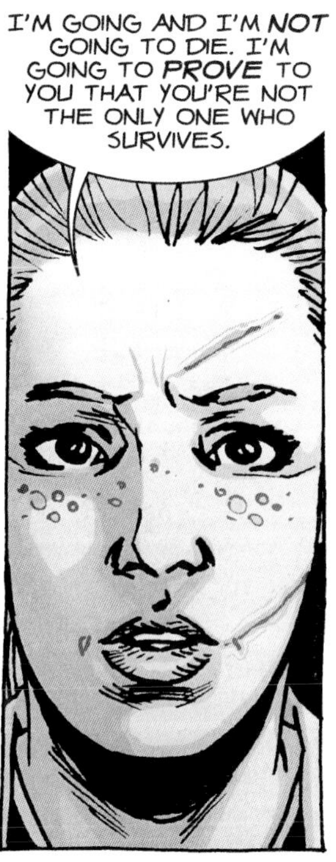
I'M GOING AND I'M *NOT* GOING TO DIE. I'M GOING TO *PROVE* TO YOU THAT YOU'RE NOT THE ONLY ONE WHO SURVIVES.

HAVEN'T YOU BEEN PAYING ATTENTION? WE'RE THE ONES THAT *LIVE,* RICK. WE'RE THE ONES WHO SURVIVE... TIME AFTER TIME, IT'S *US.*
YOU DON'T HAVE TO WORRY ABOUT ME.
DON'T MAKE ME STAY BEHIND BECAUSE YOU'RE SCARED OF WHAT MIGHT HAPPEN TO ME.
YOU *NEED* ME.

DON'T STAY AWAY TOO LONG--YOU'LL WORRY ME.
CUTE. WE'LL BE BACK HERE AS SOON AS WE CAN--AND HOPEFULLY WE'LL BE LIGHT ONE PRISONER AND LOADED DOWN WITH FOOD AND SUPPLIES.
SOUNDS GOOD TO ME.

I'LL BE CAREFUL, PROMISE.

CARL'S AT THE HOUSE--SAID HE WASN'T FEELING WELL, WANTED TO TAKE A NAP.
I HAD DOCTOR CLOYD LOOK HIM OVER, SHE SAID HE SEEMED FINE, WASN'T RUNNING A FEVER OR ANYTHING.

HE'S IN GOOD HANDS.
I'M SURE IT'S NOT AN INFECTION OR ANYTHING SERIOUS, BUT...
HE'S PROBABLY JUST WORN OUT--SOPHIA'S THE SAME WAY, SOMETIMES SHE JUST HAS TO RECHARGE. DON'T WORRY ABOUT HIM.

NEVER WANTED TO CLIMB INTO THIS THING AGAIN...

YOU READY?

KEEP AN EYE OUT--I STILL DON'T TRUST THESE PEOPLE.
I'M ON IT. WE'LL BE HERE WAITING FOR YOU WHEN YOU GET BACK.

WELL?

FOR NOW, JUST HEAD NORTH.

YOU HEARD THE MAN.

START LOOKING FOR A PLACE TO PARK IT. IT'LL BE DARK SOON.
OKAY.

TEXACO
WELL?
GOOD A PLACE AS ANY, I SUPPOSE.
HOLE UP IN THE VAN, OR SPREAD OUT INSIDE FOR THE NIGHT?
STAY CLOSE TO THE VAN, I'D SAY... JUST IN CASE WE HAVE TO LEAVE HERE IN A HURRY.

NEED HELP WITH THE PRISONER?

SURE. THIS GUY'S A SLIPPERY ONE. I COULD USE ALL THE HELP I CAN GET.

HNGH?
WAKE UP.

ARE WE THERE YET?
YOU HAVE AN ODD SENSE OF HUMOR.
SO I'VE BEEN TOLD.

DAD, I'M SORRY.
BUT--

DON'T MOVE A GODDAMN MUSCLE!
CARL, GET OUT OF THE VAN AND GET BEHIND ME--*NOW!*

RELAX, I HAVE NO INTENTION OF HURTING YOUR SON.

DAMN IT, CARL.
I DIDN'T WANT TO STAY BEHIND.

WHAT NOW? DO WE TAKE HIM BACK HOME?

DAMN IT.

GET CARL IN THE VAN-- LOCK IT UP!

SOMEONE STOP HIM!

SVAASH!

STOP OR I'LL SHOOT!

I'M TRYING TO *HELP!*
KRAK!

I CAN ONLY SLOW THEM DOWN--YOU'LL NEED TO BRAIN THEM.
WHUDD!

SHUKK!

WROKK!
BLAM!

BLAM!
PKOW!
SVAASH!

THAT... WAS IMPRESSIVE.
JUST TRYING TO DO MY PART. YOU'LL GET NO TROUBLE FROM ME.

DAD? YOU OKAY?
YEAH.

I'M SORRY I HID IN THE VAN. I JUST WANTED TO SEE THIS NEW PLACE. THAT'S ALL.
NOTHING I CAN DO ABOUT IT NOW. WE'LL DISCUSS THIS LATER.

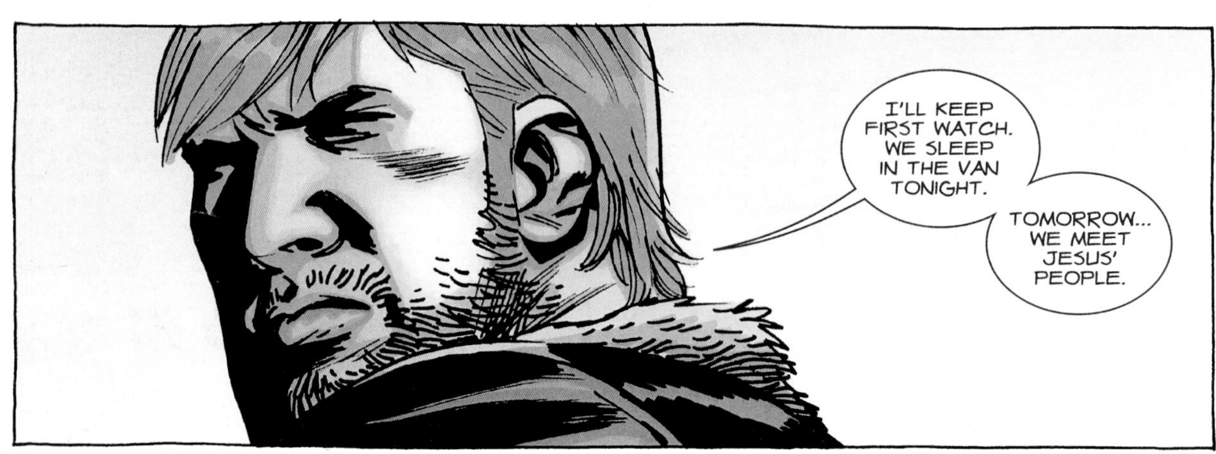
I'LL KEEP FIRST WATCH. WE SLEEP IN THE VAN TONIGHT.
TOMORROW... WE MEET JESUS' PEOPLE.

THIS ISN'T A GOOD SIGN.
SPENDING A NIGHT IN THE VAN WASN'T BAD ENOUGH? THIS *SUCKS*.

SHOULD TAKE NO MORE THAN HALF A DAY TO GET THERE FROM HERE.

THAT'S GOOD NEWS.
RIGHT?

GOING TO HAVE TO PUSH IT OFF THE ROAD.
THAT TAKES ME BACK...

WAIT.
LET ME HELP.

ALMOST.
THERE...

SHHHK!

SPLAGG!

OH MY GOD... ARE YOU OKAY?
I'M SORRY--

SORRY THAT I FELL, OR SORRY THAT YOU'VE KEPT ME TIED UP ALL THIS TIME?

THAT YOU FELL.

KEEPING YOU TIED UP, WELL... IF THIS ALTRUISTIC BIT TURNS OUT TO NOT BE AN ACT...
...DON'T EXACTLY KNOW THAT "SORRY" IS GOING TO CUT IT.

IT'D BE A GOOD START...

C'MON.

OKAY, PULL OVER.
WHAT'S WRONG?

I NEED TO GO TO THE LITTLE BOYS' ROOM.

OKAY, I'LL TAKE DOWN YOUR PANTS, BUT YOU'RE ON YOUR OWN AFTER THAT.

DON'T WORRY, I'VE GOT IT COVERED.
I MEAN, DID YOU EVER REALLY BELIEVE YOU WERE HOLDING ME PRISONER?

SO, YOU COULD HAVE FREED YOURSELF-- AT ANY TIME?
WHY DID YOU--?

I WAS TESTING YOU-- AND YOU PASSED.
I TRUSTED YOU.

IT'S YOUR SON, REALLY. I HAD A GOOD FEELING ABOUT YOU--BUT TALKING TO HIM REALLY CINCHED IT.
YOU DON'T LIVE OUT HERE FOR AS LONG AS YOU HAVE--RAISING THAT BOY TO BE THE BOY THAT HE IS... IF YOU'RE NOT GOOD PEOPLE.

THANK YOU.

WELL, NOW I NEED YOU TO RETURN THE FAVOR.
I TRUSTED YOU... NOW I NEED YOU TO DO THE SAME.

WE'RE *HERE*.
WELCOME TO THE HILLTOP.

SO THAT'S IT?

YEP.
OKAY...

SO, WHAT NOW? I'M JUST SUPPOSED TO TAKE MY PEOPLE... TRUST YOU--WALK INTO A SITUATION WHERE WE'RE GOING TO BE COMPLETELY OUTNUMBERED.
HOW COULD I DO THAT?

RICK, I LET YOU TIE ME UP, I RISKED MY LIFE TO PROVE I WASN'T A THREAT TO YOU.
I COULD HAVE ATTACKED YOU IN THE VAN, WHILE YOU WERE SLEEPING LAST NIGHT.
WHAT'S IT GOING TO TAKE?

YOU'RE JUST GOING TO HAVE TO TRUST ME.

I CAN'T... I JUST...
I'LL PUT ANDREA ON THE VAN. I'LL HAVE MICHONNE BY MY SIDE--GLENN CAN TAKE CARL SOMEWHERE SAFE. I'LL MEET YOUR BOSS, WHOEVER'S IN CHARGE--BUT HE'S GOT TO COME OUTSIDE ALONE...
THEN WHAT? YOU HOLD HIM PRISONER AND COME INSIDE? THAT'S JUST NOT GOING TO WORK, RICK. WE HAVE TO BE ABLE TO TRUST YOU, TOO.

HE'S NOT A BAD GUY, DAD.
I CAN TELL.
SO HIS PEOPLE AREN'T BAD EITHER.

OKAY.
TAKE US INSIDE.

ALL RIGHT THEN.
VAN WON'T MAKE IT UP THE HILL WITH THE GROUND SO WET. WE'LL HAVE TO WALK UP. BUT I'LL LET YOU IN ON A LITTLE SECRET--WE RAN OUT OF AMMO A WHILE BACK... AND I'M GOING TO LET YOU CARRY YOUR GUNS.

THAT MAKES ME FEEL A *LITTLE* BETTER.

MICHONNE?
ON IT.

I'M AN IDIOT. REALLY. SHE SAID SHE'S BEEN GIVING ME ALL KINDS OF SIGNALS. I DON'T EVEN KNOW WHAT THAT MEANS. LOOKING AT ME--BEING NICE? HOW AM I SUPPOSED TO PICK UP ON THAT?
WHATEVER, IT WORKED ITSELF OUT, WE'RE GOING TO HAVE DINNER TOGETHER TONIGHT. HAVE YOU MET MANDY? SHE'S--
HEADS UP, EDUARDO.

WHAT IS IT?
KAL?! IS IT NEGAN?

SHH.

WAIT, IS THAT--?

STAND DOWN, KAL--IT'S *ME!*

HAVE SOMEONE OPEN THE GATE BEFORE WE DRAW TOO MUCH ATTENTION TO OURSELVES!

JESUS, YOU KNOW I CAN'T DO THAT-- THEY'RE ARMED! TAKE THEIR GUNS BEFORE THEY TRY SOMETHING!

STAND DOWN! YOU KNOW I'M IN CHARGE OF WHO COMES IN. I VOUCH FOR THEM, THEY'RE COOL.
OPEN THE DAMN DOOR!

SORRY, THESE GUYS GET A LITTLE ANTSY, STANDING UP THERE DOING NEXT TO NOTHING ALL DAY.
THE WORST PART OF HOLDING A COOL SPEAR ALL DAY IS THAT YOU'RE JUST DYING TO ACTUALLY USE IT.

FOLLOW ME.

IMPRESSIVE, RIGHT?

YEAH.
WOW!

AS I SAID, THERE'S ALMOST TWO HUNDRED PEOPLE LIVING HERE. AT LEAST, THAT'S WHERE THINGS WERE AT WHEN I LEFT A FEW WEEKS AGO.
PROBABLY MORE NOW. HAD AT LEAST ONE PREGNANT WOMAN HERE.

THIS IS THE BARRINGTON HOUSE. EVERY ELEMENTARY SCHOOL WITHIN A FIFTY MILE RADIUS TOOK A FIELD TRIP HERE AT LEAST ONCE A YEAR.
THAT ROOM ON TOP, WHATEVER IT'S CALLED... YOU CAN SEE IN ALL DIRECTIONS FOR *MILES.* SO IT'S KIND OF PERFECT, SECURITY-WISE.

DISMANTLED PART OF THE BARN TO MAKE THE WALL?
MADE IT BIG ENOUGH TO INCLUDE THE NEARBY WATER TOWER. *NICE.*

GOT ADDITIONAL METAL SHEETING FROM OTHER BARNS AND HOUSES IN THE AREA... OR SO I WAS TOLD. PLACE WAS UP AND RUNNING BY THE TIME I GOT HERE.

THERE WERE HALF AS MANY TRAILERS HERE BACK THEN. HAD TO EXPAND A FEW MONTHS BACK.
COME ON... LET ME SHOW YOU THE HOUSE.

PLACE IS RUN PRETTY MUCH LIKE A HOTEL. MOST OF THE ROOMS HAVE BEEN CONVERTED INTO LIVING QUARTERS, EVEN THE ONES THAT WEREN'T BEDROOMS.
SOME PEOPLE PREFER TO HAVE THEIR OWN SPACE, LIKE OUT IN THE TRAILERS... OTHERS LIKE BEING TOGETHER IN ONE PLACE. FEELS SAFER.
I'LL SHOW YOU AROUND.

JESUS, WAIT...

SHOW THE REST OF THEM AROUND... I'D REALLY LIKE TO PULL ASIDE WHOEVER IS IN A POSITION OF AUTHORITY IN THIS NEW GROUP YOU'VE FOUND, BEND THEIR EAR A LITTLE.
A REAL MEETING OF THE *MINDS*.
OKAY?

I'M SORRY, GUYS--PLEASE. MEET GREGORY... HE KEEPS THE TRAINS RUNNING ON TIME AROUND HERE.
HE'S THE GUY MAKING SURE EVERYTHING IS ON THE UP AND UP.
I'M THE BOSS.

RICK'S THE GUY YOU WANT TO TALK TO, MAN.
HE'S GOOD PEOPLE, I VOUCH FOR HIM.

IT'S A PLEASURE TO MEET YOU ALL.
PLEASE, RICK. ACCOMPANY ME.

WE'LL KEEP HIM SAFE.
GO.

NICE FAMILY YOU GOT THERE, NICK.
IT'S RICK, ACTUALLY.
YEAH, YEAH... OKAY. SORRY.

SO, WHAT KIND OF PLACE YOU HOLED UP IN? NOTHING NEARLY AS NICE AS THIS, I ASSUME.
WELL, NO, BUT--
I KNOW, THIS PLACE IS PRETTY IMPRESSIVE. IT'S TAKEN A LOT OF HARD WORK ON MY PART TO MAKE THIS ALL POSSIBLE... BUT IT'S HARD WORK THAT'S REALLY PAID OFF.

YEAH.
I CAN SEE THAT.

YEAH, I'LL HAVE SOMEONE TAKE YOU AROUND, SHOW YOU ALL THAT THE HILLTOP HAS TO OFFER BEFORE DARK.
FOR NOW, TELL ME A LITTLE ABOUT YOURSELF.

WELL, I USED TO BE A POLICE OFFICER BEFORE, AND--
THERE'S A COUPLE POLICE OFFICERS HERE. I'LL INTRODUCE--

WESLEY?! WHAT'S WRONG?
IT'S ETHAN! HE'S FINALLY BACK, BUT-- IT'S JUST HIM!

C'MON, ETHAN... YOU'RE SAFE NOW.

WHERE'S DAVID, CRYSTAL AND ANDY?!
WHAT HAPPENED TO THEM?

DEAD... THEY'RE...
WAS IT NEGAN?! DID HE DO THIS?!

SAID IT WASN'T ENOUGH, SAID WE WEREN'T MEETING... OUR END OF THE BARGAIN...
THEY STILL HAVE CRYSTAL. SAID THEY'D KEEP HER ALIVE, RETURN HER TO US IF I DELIVERED A MESSAGE TO YOU...

MESSAGE?! WHAT MESSAGE?

SHUNK!
I'M SORRY.

GREGORY!
OFF ME! I HAVE TO--
WRAKK!

WRAMM!

NO!
HE HAS TO DIE! HE DIES OR CRYSTAL DIES!

HE'S BLEEDING OUT!
SOMEONE GET CARSON!

LET GO! I DON'T WANT TO HURT YOU!

SOMEONE GRAB HIM-- WHAT THE-- FUCK ARE YOU--DOING?!

STAY BACK!
ANYONE WHO TRIES TO STOP ME IS KILLING CRYSTAL!

SHLKK!

GURRGLE!
SQURRK!

UNGH.

SPUTT!

I CAN'T DO ANYTHING OUT HERE... WE NEED TO SLOW THE BLEEDING SO WE CAN MOVE HIM.
PUT YOUR HAND ON THE WOUND, APPLY PRESSURE.

DAD?

I'M FINE...

WHAT?

MY GOD! *ETHAN!*
YOU KILLED HIM!

ETHAN?
HE TRIED TO KILL GREGORY... AND ME. WHAT WAS I *SUPPOSED* TO DO?

PLEASE, RICK--YOU NEED TO UNDERSTAND THE SITUATION. I CAN EXPLAIN, THINGS AREN'T AS... *SIMPLE* AS THEY MIGHT SEEM.
JUST GIVE ME TIME.

PUT THE GUN DOWN!
NOW!

I DON'T THINK I WILL...

EVERYONE JUST CALM DOWN!
PUT YOUR WEAPONS AWAY.

I THINK YOU GUYS HAVE MORE PRESSING CONCERNS.

WE NEED TO GET HIM INSIDE, I CAN'T STOP THE BLEEDING OUT HERE--I NEED MY EQUIPMENT!
WHAT CAN I DO TO HELP?

PUT THE GUN AWAY AND LET THEM HANDLE THIS ON THEIR OWN.
YOU'VE DONE ENOUGH.

WHAT ABOUT HIM? HE'S GOING TO TURN, Y'KNOW... COULD HAPPEN SOON.
WE HAVE A PROCESS. WE'LL TAKE CARE OF IT.

SO WHAT NOW? IS RICK IN TROUBLE?
NO, OF COURSE NOT. PEOPLE JUST... THIS KIND OF THING DOESN'T USUALLY HAPPEN HERE.

WHO IS NEGAN? WHERE WOULD HE BE KEEPING CRYSTAL? I ASSUME SHE WAS ONE OF YOUR GROUP AND THIS GUY IS HOLDING HER HOSTAGE.
IF NEGAN HAS CRYSTAL SHE'S ALREADY DEAD. THERE'S NOTHING WE CAN DO FOR HER.
THERE'S A LOT YOU DON'T KNOW, I'LL... FILL YOU IN.

BUT NOT HERE.

I DON'T WANT TO SCARE THE BOY.
YOU WON'T.

OKAY, THEN...
THE SIMPLEST WAY TO PUT IT... IS THE HILLTOP HAS *ENEMIES.*

I THINK WE GATHERED THAT MUCH ON OUR OWN.

ALMOST AS SOON AS THE WALLS WERE BUILT, NEGAN SHOWED UP. HE'S THE LEADER OF A REALLY NASTY GROUP OF PEOPLE HE CALLS *THE SAVIORS.*
HE MET WITH GREGORY, MADE A LOT OF DEMANDS AND EVEN MORE *THREATS.*
GREGORY IS NOT EXACTLY GOOD AT... CONFRONTATION. I'M NOT GOING TO LIE TO YOU, HE'S NOT THE LEADER I WOULD HAVE CHOSEN, BUT THE PEOPLE LIKE HIM.
HE STRUCK A DEAL WITH THE SAVIORS.
HALF OF *EVERYTHING,* OUR SUPPLIES, OUR CROPS, OUR LIVESTOCK, BELONG TO THE SAVIORS... WE MAKE REGULAR DELIVERIES, AND THEY KEEP THE AREA RELATIVELY CLEAR OF THE DEAD.
THAT'S THE DEAL.
NEAR AS I CAN TELL, THEY'RE A ROAMING BAND OF MANIACS ON AN UNENDING KILLING SPREE... WORD IS THEY'VE KILLED THOUSANDS OF THE DEAD ALREADY.

A GUY SHOWED UP, MADE SOME THREATS, AND NOW YOU GIVE HIM HALF OF *EVERYTHING?* HOW MANY PEOPLE ARE IN THIS GROUP--THE SAVIORS?

NOBODY REALLY KNOWS...
I KNOW, IT'S SCREWED UP.

THAT'S PUTTING IT LIGHTLY. YOUR LEADER IS LETTING A GUY WHO MAY NOT EVEN BE A REAL THREAT TAKE YOUR SUPPLIES AND *TERRIFY* YOUR PEOPLE?

IT IS WHAT IT IS. GREGORY IS GOOD AT A GREAT MANY THINGS, AND OTHER THINGS... NOT SO MUCH.
THE FOOD MUST BE GOING SOMEWHERE, AND NEGAN HAS BEEN SEEN WITH GROUPS AS LARGE AS *TWENTY.*
I TRIED TRACKING THEM BACK TO THEIR HOME ONCE--THEY SAW ME, AND I BARELY ESCAPED.

IF THEY DON'T FEEL LIKE THEY'RE GETTING HALF, OR IF THEY JUST WANT TO SEND A MESSAGE, SOMETIMES THEY'LL BEAT UP THE TEAM WE SEND TO THEIR DROP POINT.
SOMETIMES *WORSE.*
LIKE TODAY.

EVERYONE HERE IS TOO SCARED TO STAND UP TO THEM...
SO WE WORK HARD, GATHERING THINGS TO HAND OVER TO THESE MADMEN... BUT IT WORKS, WE'RE SAFE, WE'RE NOT STARVING.

IF WE KILL ALL THESE BAD GUYS, WILL YOU START GIVING *US* HALF OF YOUR FOOD AND STUFF?

CONFRONTATION HAS NEVER BEEN SOMETHING WE'VE HAD A LOT OF TROUBLE WITH.
I DON'T KNOW THAT WE'D EVEN *NEED* HALF, JUST ENOUGH FOR ALL MY PEOPLE.

YOU'RE SERIOUS?
THAT SEEMS LIKE SOMETHING THAT COULD BE ARRANGED.

HEY! WHY ARE YOU HERE?! THIS IS A PRIVATE CEREMONY!
YOU'VE GOT NO RIGHT TO BE HERE!

NO RIGHT!
WRAMM!

ETHAN WAS A GOOD MAN! HE DIDN'T HAVE TO DIE!
HE WAS SCARED AND--

BACK OFF, SAMUEL! I DON'T CARE HOW MUCH WE LOVED ETHAN! HE WAS TRYING TO KILL THIS MAN!
ALL HE DID WAS DEFEND HIMSELF.

UNTIL YOU CAN CONVINCE ME NONE OF YOU WOULD HAVE DONE THE SAME-- LEAVE HIM ALONE.
ETHAN DID A BAD THING... AND HE DIED BECAUSE OF IT.

MOURN HIM BECAUSE HE'S GONE. BUT DON'T PRETEND HE WAS ANYTHING MORE THAN A COWARD WHO ATTACKED US.
HE DESERVED TO DIE.

WHAT HAPPENED TO YOUR *EYE?*

COULDN'T SLEEP LAST NIGHT, WENT OUT. I STUMBLED ACROSS A FUNERAL PYRE FOR THAT GUY WHO ATTACKED ME.
ONE OF THE MOURNERS DIDN'T APPRECIATE MY PRESENCE. BIG GUY.

UNDERSTANDABLE.
THEY CREMATE PEOPLE, HUH? THAT MAKES SENSE.

I KNOW IT'S BEEN CRAZY, BUT I'VE GOTTA BE HONEST... I *REALLY* LIKE IT HERE. THE TRAILERS AREN'T AS NICE AS OUR HOUSES, BUT THEY'VE GOT MUCH MORE LAND IN THEIR SAFE ZONE.
THERE'S MORE JOBS TO GO AROUND, MORE TO BE DONE, THE COMMUNITY SEEMS CLOSER, EVEN THOUGH IT'S LARGER. THAT'S WHY PEOPLE ARE SO UPSET OVER ETHAN, EVERYONE *KNOWS* EVERYONE HERE.
THIS PLACE IS GREAT. JUST *LOOK* AT IT.
IT'S SOMETHING SPECIAL, WON'T ARGUE WITH YOU THERE.

YOU TWO SEEM TO HAVE WOKEN UP ON THE RIGHT SIDE OF THE BED.
SOMETHING *GOOD* HAPPEN THAT I MISS?

NOTHING IN PARTICULAR...

RICK?
JUST ADMIRING THIS PLACE. IT'S A BEAUTIFUL DAY, RIGHT?

RICK?
GREGORY WOULD LIKE TO SPEAK TO YOU.

COME IN. SHUT THE DOOR BEHIND YOU.

YOU WOULDN'T **BELIEVE** HOW--AKK--PAINFUL THIS IS. FEELS LIKE SOMEONE'S TWISTING MY INSIDES WITH A MIXER--SHOOTING PAINS FROM HEAD TO--*UMPH*--TOE.
IT REALLY IS *QUITE* SEVERE.
YOU--*UNGH*--EVER HAD TO DEAL WITH SOMETHING LIKE THIS?

I'VE BEEN SHOT... ***TWICE.***
AND I LOST THE HAND.

OH... I HADN'T NOTICED.

JESUS TELLS ME YOU HAVE A PROPOSITION. YOU THINK YOU CAN ACTUALLY DEAL WITH NEGAN?
THAT'S SOMETHING WE'D BE ***VERY*** GRATEFUL FOR.

THE TRUTH OF THE MATTER IS THAT WE DON'T HAVE A LOT TO OFFER IN THE WAY OF SUPPLIES. WE'RE RUNNING LOW ON FOOD AS IT IS, WE DON'T HAVE ANYTHING TO SPARE.
SO THIS TRADE AGREEMENT THAT JESUS TOLD ME ABOUT PROBABLY WOULDN'T WORK, AT LEAST FOR NOW.
EVENTUALLY WE MAY BE ABLE TO CONTRIBUTE. BUT EVEN THEN, I DON'T KNOW HOW I'LL FEEL KNOWING HALF OF EVERYTHING I SEND HERE GOES TO A GROUP OF VIOLENT KILLERS.
NEGAN AND HIS PEOPLE HAVE BEEN A THORN IN OUR SIDE FOR SOME TIME NOW. I'VE ACCOMPLISHED AMAZING THINGS WITH THIS COMMUNITY, IT'S TRUE... BUT WE'VE NEVER BEEN STRONG ENOUGH TO FACE HIM.
ONE OF THE REASONS JESUS IS SO DILIGENT IN BRINGING NEW COMMUNITIES INTO THE FOLD IS TO LIGHTEN OUR BURDEN. MORE SOURCES OF SUPPLIES FOR THE OFFERING.
IT WAS A GOOD IDEA, BUT IT HASN'T SEEMED TO MAKE THINGS EASIER WITH NEGAN. OVER THE LAST FEW MONTHS... THINGS HAVE GOTTEN WORSE.

I'VE DEALT WITH HIS KIND BEFORE. MY PEOPLE LIVED ON THE ROAD MORE THAN OFF, FOR THE BETTER PART OF A YEAR.
WE KNOW HOW TO HANDLE PEOPLE LIKE THAT.

YOU SAYING YOU'LL FIGHT FOR US? THAT'D BE YOUR CONTRIBUTION?

IT'S AN OPTION. WE'RE DANGEROUSLY LOW ON SUPPLIES, TAKING SOMETHING BACK WITH ME WOULD GO A LONG WAY TO SWAYING MY PEOPLE TO HELP YOU.

SERIOUSLY, THANKS FOR EVERYTHING... THIS IS A MORE THAN GENEROUS OFFERING.

RICK, IF I DIDN'T KNOW BETTER, I'D SAY YOU'RE STARTING TO TRUST US...

IT'S NOT EASY TO EARN, BUT ONCE YOU SUCCEED IN GAINING MY TRUST, IT'S APPRECIATED AND ALWAYS RECOGNIZED.
THIS FOOD IS GOING TO GET US THROUGH THE REST OF WINTER. THAT WON'T BE FORGOTTEN.

WHEN THE TIME COMES TO GO AGAINST NEGAN, YOU CAN EXPECT KAL AND ME BY YOUR SIDE... AS WELL AS OTHERS.
WE WOULDN'T WANT YOU TO FACE THEM ALONE.

WHAT IS HE TALKING ABOUT?
WE'RE GOING TO HELP THEM DEAL WITH THIS NEGAN GUY.
YOU VOLUNTEERED US FOR THAT?
NO. I'M GOING TO TRY AND TALK YOU INTO IT, LATER. NOT NOW.

IT'S THE RIGHT THING TO DO.

WELL, I'LL LEAVE YOU TO IT. I SUPPOSE WE'LL BE IN TOUCH.
WE WILL.

ARE YOU REALLY SERIOUS ABOUT THIS?

WHAT, ANDREA-- ABOUT HELPING THESE PEOPLE? OF COURSE I AM!
YOU HAVE A PROBLEM WITH IT?!
I FEEL LUCKY WE MADE IT OUT OF THERE ALIVE. THEY'RE LED BY A CULT LEADER, THEY GIVE OFFERINGS TO MURDERERS...
THEY WERE TERRIFYING. DID YOU JUST NOT NOTICE?
THEY WERE SCARED OUT OF THEIR MINDS WHEN THEIR LEADER WAS ATTACKED. MOST WERE SO FROZEN THEY COULDN'T EVEN HELP.
THOSE PEOPLE WERE PATHETIC.

WHAT?

PEOPLE HAVE BEEN LOOKING TO ME FOR ANSWERS, PRETTY MUCH SINCE DAY ONE... I WAS NEVER ASKED IF I WANTED TO BE A LEADER, EVERYONE JUST STARTED EXPECTING ME TO FILL THAT ROLE.
SOMETIMES I THINK ABOUT WHY. MOST OF THE TIME I JUST ASSUME IT MUST BE BECAUSE OF MY PAST AS A POLICE OFFICER, WHICH ALWAYS AMUSED ME.
THE FACT IS, I WAS NEVER ALL THAT GOOD.

I KNOW THE FACT THAT I'M A FATHER IS A BIG PART OF IT, MY DRIVE TO PROTECT MY FAMILY HAS ALWAYS HELPED THOSE AROUND ME.
BUT THAT'S NOT "IT."

I'VE BEEN AT THIS FOR A GOOD LONG TIME, BUT IT WASN'T UNTIL NOW THAT I PINPOINTED... "IT."
THE REASON I WAS MADE LEADER.

IT'S THE WAY I SEE THINGS.

WE ALL SAW THE HILLTOP TOGETHER.
YOU SAW SOMETHING TO LOVE.
SOMETHING TO RIDICULE.
SOMETHING TO FEAR.
I SAW THE FUTURE. NOT A PERFECT PLACE, NOT BY A LONG SHOT. BUT IT'S A FOUNDATION... THE START OF SOMETHING... HISTORIC.
THOSE PEOPLE IN THERE DON'T LIVE IN FEAR, THEY DON'T WORRY ABOUT WHAT'S ON THE OUTSIDE OF THAT WALL. FRANKLY, THEY ARE COMPLETELY INCAPABLE OF DEALING WITH ANYTHING FROM OUTSIDE.
THEY JUST LIVE.
THIS IS A SPECIAL PLACE, MADE EVEN MORE SPECIAL BY THE FACT THAT THEY NEED US. THEY NEED OUR SKILLS, OUR CAPABILITIES. WE CAN BE THE BACKBONE OF THIS NETWORK THEY'VE BUILT.
THEY'VE GOT NEARLY TWO HUNDRED PEOPLE... WE CAN TURN THEM INTO AN ARMY.
AN ARMY TO PROTECT US FROM ANYONE WHO WOULD MEAN TO DO US HARM... BUT ALSO AN ARMY TO ACTUALLY FACE THIS UNDEAD MENACE HEAD ON... REALLY DO SOMETHING ABOUT IT.

I SEE A WORLD WITHOUT ROAMERS... A WORLD WHERE CHILDREN PLAY IN THESE FIELDS...
...A WORLD WHERE WE DON'T HAVE TO BE SCARED ANYMORE.
I KNOW I'M NOT THE ONLY ONE OF US WHO SOMETIMES WONDERS-- WHY? WHY EVEN BOTHER... WITH SO MUCH DEATH AROUND US, SO MUCH LOSS, WHY GO ON?
WE'VE LOST OUR WIVES, MOTHERS, SISTERS, LOVERS, FRIENDS... THAT'S PAIN ENOUGH TO CRIPPLE SOMEONE, AND YET, WE CARRY ON.
WHY DO WE CONTINUE TO SURVIVE DESPITE IT ALL?

THIS IS WHY. THIS PLACE.
THIS IS WHAT WE'VE BEEN LIVING FOR. ALL OUR STRUGGLES AND HARD WORK HAVE BEEN LEADING TO THIS.

WE'VE BEEN SURVIVING IN ORDER TO REACH THIS MOMENT, THIS DISCOVERY. THE HILLTOP... THIS IS OUR FUTURE.
WE CAN REBUILD CIVILIZATION NOW. WE'RE ONE STEP CLOSER TO GETTING BACK TO THE WAY THINGS WERE BEFORE.
WE CAN BE AT PEACE AGAIN.
WE CAN RAISE OUR CHILDREN AGAIN.
WE CAN LOVE OUR FAMILIES AGAIN.

WE CAN LET OUR GUARD DOWN AGAIN.
WHATEVER HARDSHIP COMES OUT OF THIS AGREEMENT... IT WILL BE WORTH IT.

THIS CHANGES EVERYTHING. CAN'T YOU SEE THAT?
WE CAN FINALLY STOP SURVIVING...
...AND START LIVING.

to be continued...

Sketchbook

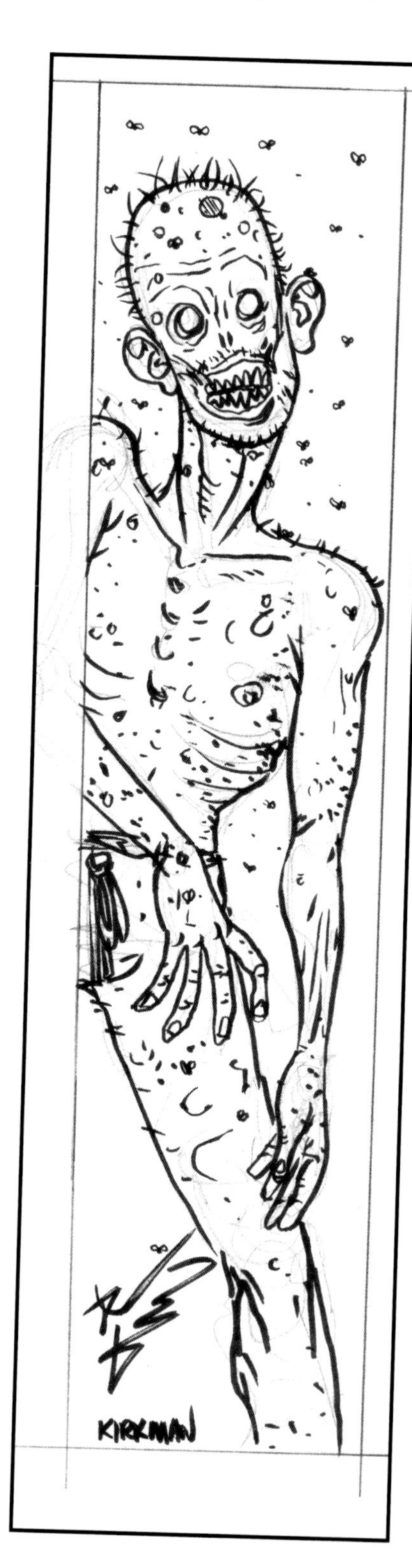

We did some special limited edition watches with a company called Vannen Watches that were totally awesome. To make things a little more special, Vannen had the idea to put original drawings from me and Charlie inserted randomly into two packages. Charlie drew this awesome Michonne--and I drew this terrible zombie. I saw Charlie's Michonne on ebay a matter of days after the watch was released. I don't remember ever hearing about anyone finding my zombie. I swear that business in his crotch area is supposed to be the drawstring on a pair of sweatpants... you didn't have to throw my drawing away, random fan. That was harsh, man!

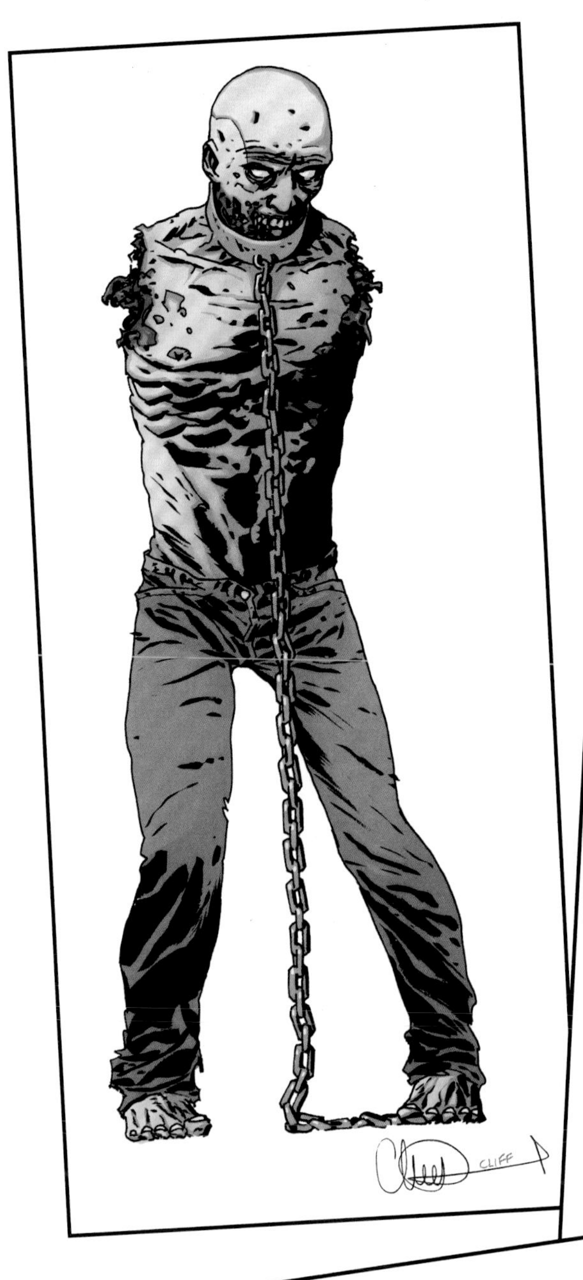

These are some random zombies drawn by Charlie and colored by Cliff that were used for signing plates in the limited editioned signed versions of the omnibus hardcovers. So... not so special now, are they?! You're seeing them RIGHT HERE!

This is an older illustration of Michonne that was used for the IMAGE EXPO variant of Walking Dead issue #idon'tremember. I like to picture a busted fire hydrant below them. Cool, right?

These illustrations were done for the limited edition MICHONNE action figure from McFarlane Toys & Skybound, which included her poncho that we sold at Comic-Con in 2012. We later used the larger illustration as the cover to the MICHONNE SPECIAL, which was timed with the launch of season 3 of the TV show. The special reprinted issue 19 (her first appearance) and her origin story which first appeared in that one issue of Playboy. It's paragraphs like this that I never thought I'd write; my life has gotten pretty crazy thanks to The Walking Dead. As I write this, I'm in a hotel in Georgia, waking up at the crack of late-afternoon, after a late night of filiming on season 3 that involved a ton of gunfire. Sorry, Georgia residents!

So, I had this idea for the cover of 95, that our group would be impressed by the massive wall around the Hilltop... and the cover would be them looking up at it, impressed. Well, it didn't really work. It looked like they were seeing a space ship. So my terrible idea just ended up wasting Charlie's and Cliff's time. You can't win them all! Sorry guys!

This Rick illustration was used for the cover of a limited edition hardcover of the Compendium One book that collects the first 48 issues of this series in one painfully heavy volume. This yellow zombie is for the cover of the fourth deluxe hardcover (sometimes called an Omnibus) y'know... the slipcased ones. Neat, right?

The splattered zombie done as a variant cover for Fan Expo Canada... I really dig this cover, it's a cool zombie. The below spread is from an old issue, but we had Cliff color it up so we'd have another awesome zombie image to use in places. It's totally cool seeing a previously black and white page from the book in color. Really cool.

This rad painting was done by Charlie for the Image Comics 2011 comic-con yearbook. It was used somewhere else as I recall (because we recycle a lot) but I can't remember where... oh, wait... Image Expo program cover? Maybe... something like that.

Oh, this is the cover of THE WALKING DEAD: CUTTING ROOM FLOOR hardcover. That thing printed all my various hand-written plots for this series... and had commentary from me discussing plot threads I altered or completely abandoned and how the story of this series evolves as I write it. That book was awesome, wasn't it?

This image was used as part of the Image/Skybound booth at Comic-Con, there's an Invincible image on one side of it and Thief of Thieves on the other side. It was really weird seeing all the vastly different Skybound books together in one image. Awesome coloring by John Rauch, though.

REGAL
CLIFF

CLIFF

MORE GREAT BOOKS FROM ROBERT KIRKMAN & SKYBOUND!

THE ASTOUNDING WOLF-MAN

VOL. 1 TP
ISBN: 978-1-58240-862-0
$14.99

VOL. 2 TP
ISBN: 978-1-60706-007-9
$14.99

VOL. 3 TP
ISBN: 978-1-60706-111-3
$16.99

VOL. 4 TP
ISBN: 978-1-60706-249-3
$16.99

BATTLE POPE

VOL. 1: GENESIS TP
ISBN: 978-1-58240-572-8
$14.99

VOL. 2: MAYHEM TP
ISBN: 978-1-58240-529-2
$12.99

VOL. 3: PILLOW TALK TP
ISBN: 978-1-58240-677-0
$12.99

VOL. 4: WRATH OF GOD TP
ISBN: 978-1-58240-751-7
$9.99

BRIT

VOL. 1: OLD SOLDIER TP
ISBN: 978-1-58240-678-7
$14.99

VOL. 2: AWOL
ISBN: 978-1-58240-864-4
$14.99

VOL. 3: FUBAR
ISBN: 978-1-60706-061-1
$16.99

CAPES

VOL. 1: PUNCHING THE CLOCK TP
ISBN: 978-1-58240-756-2
$17.99

HAUNT

VOL. 1 TP
ISBN: 978-1-60706-154-0
$9.99

VOL. 2 TP
ISBN: 978-1-60706-229-5
$16.99

VOL. 3 TP
ISBN: 978-1-60706-552-4
$14.99

THE IMMORTAL EDITION, VOL. 1 HC
ISBN: 978-1-60706-241-7
$34.99

THE INFINITE

VOL. 1 TP
ISBN: 978-1-60706-475-6
$9.99

INVINCIBLE

VOL. 1: FAMILY MATTERS TP
ISBN: 978-1-58240-711-1
$12.99

VOL. 2: EIGHT IS ENOUGH TP
ISBN: 978-1-58240-347-2
$12.99

VOL. 3: PERFECT STRANGERS TP
ISBN: 978-1-58240-793-7
$12.99

VOL. 4: HEAD OF THE CLASS TP
ISBN: 978-1-58240-440-2
$14.95

VOL. 5: THE FACTS OF LIFE TP
ISBN: 978-1-58240-554-4
$14.99

VOL. 6: A DIFFERENT WORLD TP
ISBN: 978-1-58240-579-7
$14.99

VOL. 7: THREE'S COMPANY TP
ISBN: 978-1-58240-656-5
$14.99

VOL. 8: MY FAVORITE MARTIAN TP
ISBN: 978-1-58240-683-1
$14.99

VOL. 9: OUT OF THIS WORLD TP
ISBN: 978-1-58240-827-9
$14.99

VOL. 10: WHO'S THE BOSS TP
ISBN: 978-1-60706-013-0
$16.99

VOL. 11: HAPPY DAYS TP
ISBN: 978-1-60706-062-8
$16.99

VOL. 12: STILL STANDING TP
ISBN: 978-1-60706-166-3
$16.99

VOL. 13: GROWING PAINS TP
ISBN: 978-1-60706-251-6
$16.99

VOL. 14: THE VILTRUMITE WAR TP
ISBN: 978-1-60706-367-4
$19.99

VOL. 15: GET SMART TP
ISBN: 978-1-60706-498-5
$16.99

VOL. 16: FAMILY TIES TP
ISBN: 978-1-60706-579-1
$16.99

ULTIMATE COLLECTION, VOL. 1 HC
ISBN 978-1-58240-500-1
$34.95

ULTIMATE COLLECTION, VOL. 2 HC
ISBN: 978-1-58240-594-0
$34.99

ULTIMATE COLLECTION, VOL. 3 HC
ISBN: 978-1-58240-763-0
$34.99

ULTIMATE COLLECTION, VOL. 4 HC
ISBN: 978-1-58240-989-4
$34.99

ULTIMATE COLLECTION, VOL. 5 HC
ISBN: 978-1-60706-116-8
$34.99

ULTIMATE COLLECTION, VOL. 6 HC
ISBN: 978-1-60706-360-5
$34.99

ULTIMATE COLLECTION, VOL. 7 HC
ISBN: 978-1-60706-509-8
$39.99

THE OFFICIAL HANDBOOK OF THE INVINCIBLE UNIVERSE TP
ISBN: 978-1-58240-831-6
$12.99

INVINCIBLE PRESENTS, VOL. 1: ATOM EVE & REX SPLODE TP
ISBN: 978-1-60706-255-4
$14.99

THE COMPLETE INVINCIBLE LIBRARY, VOL. 2 HC
ISBN: 978-1-60706-112-0
$125.00

THE COMPLETE INVINCIBLE LIBRARY, VOL. 3 HC
ISBN: 978-1-60706-421-3
$125.00

INVINCIBLE COMPENDIUM VOL. 1
ISBN: 978-1-60706-411-4
$64.99

THE WALKING DEAD

VOL. 1: DAYS GONE BYE TP
ISBN: 978-1-58240-672-5
$9.99

VOL. 2: MILES BEHIND US TP
ISBN: 978-1-58240-775-3
$14.99

VOL. 3: SAFETY BEHIND BARS TP
ISBN: 978-1-58240-805-7
$14.99

VOL. 4: THE HEART'S DESIRE TP
ISBN: 978-1-58240-530-8
$14.99

VOL. 5: THE BEST DEFENSE TP
ISBN: 978-1-58240-612-1
$14.99

VOL. 6: THIS SORROWFUL LIFE TP
ISBN: 978-1-58240-684-8
$14.99

VOL. 7: THE CALM BEFORE TP
ISBN: 978-1-58240-828-6
$14.99

VOL. 8: MADE TO SUFFER TP
ISBN: 978-1-58240-883-5
$14.99

VOL. 9: HERE WE REMAIN TP
ISBN: 978-1-60706-022-2
$14.99

VOL. 10: WHAT WE BECOME TP
ISBN: 978-1-60706-075-8
$14.99

VOL. 11: FEAR THE HUNTERS TP
ISBN: 978-1-60706-181-6
$14.99

VOL. 12: LIFE AMONG THEM TP
ISBN: 978-1-60706-254-7
$14.99

VOL. 13: TOO FAR GONE TP
ISBN: 978-1-60706-329-2
$14.99

VOL. 14: NO WAY OUT TP
ISBN: 978-1-60706-392-6
$14.99

VOL. 15: WE FIND OURSELVES TP
ISBN: 978-1-60706-392-6
$14.99

BOOK ONE HC
ISBN: 978-1-58240-619-0
$34.99

BOOK TWO HC
ISBN: 978-1-58240-698-5
$34.99

BOOK THREE HC
ISBN: 978-1-58240-825-5
$34.99

BOOK FOUR HC
ISBN: 978-1-60706-000-0
$34.99

BOOK FIVE HC
ISBN: 978-1-60706-171-7
$34.99

BOOK SIX HC
ISBN: 978-1-60706-327-8
$34.99

BOOK SEVEN HC
ISBN: 978-1-60706-439-8
$34.99

BOOK EIGHT HC
ISBN: 978-1-60706-593-7
$34.99

DELUXE HARDCOVER, VOL. 1
ISBN: 978-1-58240-619-0
$100.00

DELUXE HARDCOVER, VOL. 2
ISBN: 978-1-60706-029-7
$100.00

DELUXE HARDCOVER, VOL. 3
ISBN: 978-1-60706-330-8
$100.00

THE WALKING DEAD: THE COVERS, VOL. 1 HC
ISBN: 978-1-60706-002-4
$24.99

THE WALKING DEAD SURVIVORS' GUIDE
ISBN: 978-1-60706-458-9
$12.99

SUPER DINOSAUR

VOL. 1
ISBN: 978-1-60706-420-6
$9.99

VOL. 2
ISBN: 978-1-60706-568-5
$12.99

DELUXE COLORING BOOK
ISBN: 978-1-60706-481-7
$4.99

SUPERPATRIOT

AMERICA'S FIGHTING FORCE
ISBN: 978-1-58240-355-1
$14.99

TALES OF THE REALM

HARDCOVER
ISBN: 978-1-58240-426-0
$34.95

TRADE PAPERBACK
ISBN: 978-1-58240-394-6
$14.95

TECH JACKET

VOL. 1: THE BOY FROM EARTH TP
ISBN: 978-1-58240-771-5
$14.99

THIEF OF THIEVES

VOL. 1
ISBN: 978-1-60706-592-0
$14.99

WITCH DOCTOR

VOL. 1: UNDER THE KNIFE TP
ISBN: 978-1-60706-441-1
$12.99

TO FIND YOUR NEAREST COMIC BOOK STORE, CALL:
1-888-COMIC-BOOK